Destiny Series

Five Novelettes With A Twist

Casi McLean

Dedication

This book is dedicated to my brother Al, who, even as a child, dreamed of writing incredible fantasy worlds and enchanting characters he created. He never realized that dream. After suffering a massive stroke, he passed away last year, but I like to think he's dancing with my muse as I pen my stories.

The Destiny Series

Award-winning Destiny, was a winner in the
AWC's 2013 Writing Contest.

Below are the judges' comments:

At first these stories reel you in to what appears to be a
formula romance. Then they turn the genre on its head,
throwing a perfectly aimed, delightful curveball at the
surprising and satisfying end. The writer doesn't rush any
part of the story, letting the reader see, hear, and feel the
magical eeriness of one fateful night

Thank you for your interest in my books.

Please visit me on the Internet:

My website: casimclean.com
Casi McLean on Amazon.com
Casi McLean on Goodreads.com
Follow me on Twitter @casimclean
And "Like" Casi McLean-Author on Facebook

Destiny

Book One

Casi McLean

Destiny

"Save my daddy." The child's soft voice whispered across the mist.

Reagan leaned forward, stilling the movement of her porch swing and squinted to see through the deepening haze hovering over the water. Surely she imagined the whimpers. Perhaps the cries came from a raccoon or the squeak of the pontoon bumpers rubbing against the dock.

There was no way a child could wander this far from civilization. Reagan hadn't seen a soul since she arrived at her cabin retreat, except when she drove into town for groceries. And that's the way she wanted it. She'd searched out the solitude of Hidden Cove, an isolated inlet on Spirit Lake near the mouth of the Chattahoochee with ten miles of forest between her and the closest neighbor. There wasn't even a cell tower close enough to pick up a signal without driving a few miles down the old dirt road that led to her cottage.

Reagan stood, tucking her long blonde hair behind her ears, and listened to the hush of the secluded harbor. She loved this time of the evening, when the sun slipped into the horizon and nocturnal animals scurried through the underbrush. But tonight, an unsettling energy hung in the air shaded in silent stillness.

Goose bumps ran down her arms. She brushed her palms across them and reached for the throw draped over the back of the swing. It wasn't like her to be oversensitive. Nestling back into her seat she tried to relax, but faint weeping broke the quiet, followed by the timid plea.

"Save my daddy."

Tossing the blanket aside, she pushed off of the swing and grabbed the flashlight she'd hung on a nail next to the door. This time, there was no mistaking the child's anguish.

"Where are you?" Reagan crept down the steps, plodding toward the lake and the source of the desperate lament. She gazed across the water shrouded in eerie fog, then toward the twilight sky. A full moon veiled by wispy clouds cast an anomalous glow through the tall trees that dissolved into blackness as it pierced the strange haze cloaking the water. An icy shiver ran down her spine coaxed further by the cool, October air.

She'd been staying in the cabin for almost six weeks now, had lived near water most of her life, but never had she experienced such an unnerving feeling. Flipping on her flashlight, she scanned the path ahead. The familiar lapping of the lake at dusk always calmed her. She basked in its subtle serenity. But the lagoon felt ominous tonight, like an evil presence lurked somewhere beyond the shoreline masked by the murky haze. She couldn't bear the thought of a child wandering aimlessly through the woods, lost and alone.

That's how she had felt for the last few months, lost and alone. Sometimes she wished she had never rummaged through the attic looking for that stupid book. What was so important about The Velveteen Rabbit anyway? Why didn't she simply purchase a new copy instead of dwelling on the "sentimental" value of the gift? If she hadn't combed through the attic, she'd never found her mother's diary, never seen the birth certificate. She'd still be living in sweet ignorance, oblivious that her entire life––twenty-three years––had been a continuous deception. Not that she had a problem with adoption. It was the secrets and lies that tormented her.

Soft sobs brought her back to the moment. She strained to see, tramping through brushwood, her heart pounding. Moonlight glimmered between the branches, catching locks of the child's golden hair as she darted behind a tree before cautiously peering around the trunk.

"I won't hurt you." Reagan held out her hand to the little girl, but the child scurried further into the woods. She couldn't be more than five or six. What in the world was such a young child doing wandering in the middle of nowhere?

"Please come back. I want to help you." Trudging forward, Reagan followed the little girl, seeing only a glimpse of her hair or a flash of the child's white pinafore scooting between the trees and foliage.

The sound of water splashing on the shore grew louder and Reagan knew the lake lay dead ahead. She rushed forward. "I'll help you find your daddy if you just stop."

"He's not lost."

Startled, Reagan spun around to see the little girl standing directly behind her. Dressed in a pristine white cotton dress, lacey anklets and white paten-leather shoes, she stared at the ground, her golden hair draping her shoulders in ringlets. Reagan stooped down, bent her finger and lifted the child's chin. When the little girl looked up, her deep violet eyes reached into Reagan's soul and a smile washed across her face.

"What's your name, Sweetie?"

"Des ...tin ...y."

"It's nice to meet you. I'm Reagan."

Destiny smiled briefly then scrunched her brow. "Daddy's not lost." She lowered her chin again. "He needs help."

"Where is he?"

The little girl looked up at Reagan with a hopeful gaze. "I can show you."

"I don't think wandering through these woods is such a great idea right now. Especially near the lake. I've never seen such a creepy haze over the water." Reagan held out her hand to the child. "Why don't we go back to my house for a while. You can tell me what happened to your daddy and we'll figure out the best way to help him."

"Please." She grabbed Reagan's wrist and tugged with the full weight of her tiny body. "Daddy might be hurt."

Drenched in moonlight, the child's eyes beckoned with a mesmeric glamour, charming Reagan into compliance. But the closer they moved toward the lake, the lingering sense of latent evil intensified and her protective instincts heightened.

Destiny maneuvered through the forest, weaving in and out of the lush undergrowth with the cool confidence of a seasoned woodsman. When the foul odor of rotting fish and dank earth flooded the air, a wave of dread consumed Reagan. She could see only darkness, but had no doubt the lake lay beneath the fog. Destiny halted, pointing into the murk.

"There." She gazed up at Reagan. "Daddy is out there."

"In the water?" Reagan gasped at the thought. If Des's father was on the lake, how could they ever find him? Catching a glimpse of an odd towering image, Reagan strained to see more clearly, then, with Des in tow, strode along the shoreline for a better view.

Sycamore and oak branches, interspersed with tall Georgia pines stretched across the cove like fingers pressing the mist into the watery depths. What appeared to be an old wooden mast pierced through the hovering fog toward the hazy moon.

"Impossible. Reagan glared at the image. "There's no way a ship could navigate into Spirit Lake." She stooped down, taking Destiny's hands into hers. "Is your daddy on a boat?

"Yes. I saw him walk toward the big pole but he fell down and didn't get up." She peered up at her new companion, pleading. "He must be hurt. Please, you've got to save him."

Reagan's gaze shifted from the child to the mysterious shadow beyond the shore. The mast teetered back and forth, rocking gently as the vessel drifted. She could see the outline now, a sleek, narrow hull with a sharp bow. The image looked as if it was yanked from the pages of history.

With a furrowed brow, she shook her head to dismiss the odd sense of surreal reality that crept over her. The eerie mist hovering over the lake, an antiquated mast stabbing through the fog into the night sky, a small child wandering though the forest miles from the nearest town--nothing made sense, least of all a nineteenth century sloop inexplicably adrift in Spirit Lake. The shallow coastline and unpredictable flow of the Chattahoochee made the route impossible. No craft of that size had ventured north of Columbus in over a century.

Reagan glared through the haze. She could see the dock now, her dock. Somehow, amidst the mystery and meandering, they had circled back. She heard the familiar lapping that had lulled her to sleep for the past six weeks. The pontoon creaked with the rhythmic current as the boat nudged against wooden pylons.

Her cottage stood just around the embankment only a few hundred yards away, but the mist broached the shoreline like viscous ooze creeping inland, swallowing everything in its path. At first the evil presence emanating from the lake was contained, hovering only over the water, but now the miasma breached her harbor, enveloped her haven.

Attempting to drive her Camry on the winding roads in dense fog would be far too dangerous. How could she "save" the little girl's father without help? At the moment her seclusion didn't seem like such a bright idea after all. But there was no time to dwell on past decisions. A man's life could be in jeopardy. Clasping Destiny's hand tighter, Reagan pressed forward.

"Where are we going?" Des nuzzled close to her new friend.

"To my cabin, but don't worry." She slowed, bent down and scooped Des onto her hip. "I have an idea."

"To save Daddy?"

"Yes, but you have to trust me, okay, Sweetie?"

Des smiled and threw her arms around Reagan's neck, snuggling her head into the crook. "I do."

Steering toward the mast would be fairly easy. Reagan could navigate the pontoon with her eyes closed and in such thick fog she would be doing exactly that. But she knew the sounds of Hidden Cove. She'd have little problem pulling the boat alongside the ship and finding a way to board the vessel. Her nautical instincts made her a skillful mariner. But she couldn't drag the child along. There had to be a way to keep the little girl safe while she slipped away to investigate the mysterious illusion.

How long was Des wandering the forest? She had to be hungry, tired and so scared. A good meal and reassurance was a start, but how would Reagan protect Des in her absence? Thoughts churned through her mind as she rubbed the little girl's back, intuitively comforting her.

The moon peeked between increasing clouds, casting shadowy images through naked branches onto the pathway. Reagan's flashlight flickered and dimmed. New batteries, she thought. She would replace them before she left the house again.

"This is where I live." She carried Des up the front steps to the screen door. "Are you hungry?"

Des raised her head, shook it up and down.

"You sit here"--Reagan plopped the child onto a wicker bar stool--"and we'll see what we can find in the fridge." She pulled out a carton of milk, some leftover mac and cheese and a bowl of sliced strawberries she had for breakfast that morning.

"Will this do?" She placed the pasta and fruit on the counter.

"Mmm." Des licked her lips, reaching for the berries.

"Hold on a second." Reagan chuckled. "Let's clean you up first. Lord only knows what kind of muck you may have picked up running through the woods." She grabbed a hand towel, drenched it under the faucet and squeezed a few drops of soap on one side before wiping Des's hands and face, then tossed the towel next to the sink.

For as long as she could remember, a scoop of warm, cheesy macaroni and sliced strawberries had been comfort food for Reagan and she felt a congenial sense of satisfaction knowing they enticed Des as well. Nourishment ...check. The next step would be reassurance. She had already gained the child's confidence and despite the creepy ambiance engulfing the lake tonight, the little girl captured her curiosity--and her heart.

The whole ordeal must have taken its toll on Des. She was unquestionably exhausted. Convincing the child to lie down and sleep wouldn't be difficult, but making sure she stayed asleep was a different matter. Reagan's eyes drifted to the bottle of vanilla vodka next to the sink. Her latest indulgence was chocolate martinis. A touch of vodka in a cup of hot cocoa might ...no ...she couldn't intoxicate a child? That was unthinkable, wasn't it? Perhaps, but Grams had given whiskey to her children when they were teething. She said it helped them sleep. It would be far worse if Des woke up and wandered away in this spooky fog, wouldn't it? A little splash of vodka might relax the child enough to insure Reagan at least a few hours to investigate the ship.

She looked at Des who was finishing her last bite of macaroni. "What do you say we go sit on the sofa and have some graham crackers and a cup of hot chocolate for desert?"

"With marshmallows?" Des's violet eyes sparkled.

"Of course." Reagan smiled. Being a chocoholic finally came in handy. She loved s'mores and made sure to keep a supply of graham crackers, chocolate bars and marshmallows on hand at all times. "So, what were you and your daddy doing out in these woods?" Reagan grabbed the crackers, mixed her concoction, then handed the potion to Des and sat down beside her.

"Daddy was vestigating dirty water."

"You mean 'investigating?'"

"Yes. That's when he found the boat. I was watching him from the beach."

There was something about this little girl that mesmerized Reagan. She'd do what ever it took to find the child's father.

"I'll go help your daddy, but you have to promise me something first." She stroked Destiny's hair. "Promise you'll stay here and sleep until I get back."

Des yawned and snuggled closer. "I promise." Her sleepy voice came out in a whisper.

Reagan glanced at her watch, 8:20. She slipped off Des's shoes and set them beside the front door. "I'll let you snuggle with my favorite blanket. It's so soft." She carried the child into the bedroom and tucked her in.

Confident she had at least a few hours to unravel the mystery before Destiny would stir, Reagan grabbed the boat keys, stuffed them into her jeans pocket, then picked up the flashlight and crept out the door. She solved one dilemma, but the one that loomed before her was far more daunting.

The murky fog had grown so dense she felt it slither down her throat with each inhalation. The blanket swallowed the light emanating from her cabin before she reached the dock and blotted out the moon that had shown through the trees only an hour earlier. With rote precision, she made her way through darkness toward the timber mooring's rhythmic chant. But the murmur emanating from the lake she loved had shifted from enticing to ominous.

"Destiny ...focus on Destiny and finding her father," Reagan whispered. She strode forward, clinging to each pylon to steady herself. When she reached for the boat rail, the pontoon tugged at its fetters, pulling as if some magnetic force averted Reagan's grasp. Tightening her grip, she propelled herself forward vaulting over the railing and onto the craft.

The seat cushions broke her impact, but the flashlight flew from her hand. She felt her way to the ropes, untied the knots then, fumbling for the keys, made her way to the ignition and started the engine.

The pontoon lights glowed but did little for visibility. She flipped them off. A stealth approach might facilitate the rescue, especially since she had no idea what she was getting herself into. The ship was only a few hundred yards from her dock, but unanchored it may have drifted.

Reagan could see little through the eerie gloom. She slowed to a crawl, listening to every splash and surge. The last thing she needed was to crash into the vessel. With an increasing sense of impending doom, she shuddered, but Destiny's anguish niggled at her, coercing her forward despite her own fears.

As the pontoon drifted closer, the drone hum of muted voices--hundreds of them--emerged from deep within the hull, a crooning that raised the hairs on the back of her neck. And a dank, foul odor hung over the water surrounding the craft. Killing the engine, she choked back the urge to retch. The boat floated toward the incessant murmurs until the bumpers kissed the structure. With the soft thud something jarred loose, spiraled across the carpet and spun into Reagan's ankle. The impact stung, and she instinctively reached for her foot, biting her tongue to keep from making a sound.

When the throbbing eased, she felt around the floor for the culprit. The flashlight. Thank God. Flipping it on, she instantly realized she'd forgotten to replace the batteries. But the illumination, though dim, would last for a while. The weak light had to suffice. She'd come too far to return to the cabin for such a minor detail.

Reagan edged the pontoon along side the wooden stern. Adrift on the cove there would be no gangplank, but she'd find a way to get aboard. Restarting the engine to troll the perimeter would alert the crew, so she pushed against the larger vessel with her bare hands to avoid discovery, searching for an entry point. Ebony mist surrounding her, she still could see very little, but her eyes slowly adjusted to the darkness. If only she could find an open portal, a cargo door or rigging of some kind.

She eased her way along side the sloop toward the bow until she finally found several ropes ranging in circumference from the size of her thumb to nearly seven inches in diameter. They plunged from the deck above into the water. After tying her pontoon securely to the twine, she threw the keys in the glove compartment and gazed up at the giant wooden mast towering against looming shadows, at least forty feet from its base to the peak.

The crew's whispers intensified from deep within the bowels of the ship causing the knot inside Reagan's stomach to tighten. Despite their eerie murmurs, it was more likely they'd gathered to celebrate as opposed to discussing illicit intentions.

Perhaps relishing their success in forging such a risky voyage. Whatever the reason, she hoped they'd be distracted by the festivities. If she could climb the ropes up to the deck, she'd have a good chance of finding Des's father and escaping without being discovered ...odd she kept referring to the man that way. She'd never even asked the child her Daddy's name.

Reagan tugged on the heavy twine to be sure it would hold her weight. Her athleticism sucked, but she could do this. She'd scaled the footholds at the rock climbing gym numerous times in an attempt to impress Brian, her most recent infatuation. He was hot, but like all of the men she dated, the connection was shallow, passionless. At least she learned a beneficial skill though the involvement.

She opened the glove compartment again in search of something to protect her palms. Duct tape. That would work. It might be a bit slippery, but it would help keep the skin on her hands from tearing against the rough twine. She took a deep breath then blew out before attempting to scale the bow. Shimming awkwardly to the deck, she hoisting herself over the rail.

She hid behind a bulkhead and gazed around, but saw no one, so she slunk between the shadows exploring the surface, her senses on high alert. The ship was antiquated, yet the pristine condition of the vessel suggested otherwise, as if it were plucked from the 1840s and gently deposited into Spirit Lake. Elaborate carvings were etched into the wood at various intervals, like some kind of hieroglyphics.

Reagan stole around the deck, looking for any sign of life beyond that of the dismal hum emanating from beneath. She couldn't shake the intense awareness of evil surrounding her, a feeling she'd had from the moment the mist rolled inland. There was nothing evil about Destiny, though. Every instinct Reagan possessed screamed for her to do whatever she could to help the child.

So far, the vessel appeared to be deserted––except for the unremitting whispers echoing from below. Drawn toward the clamor, she followed the murmurs down a staircase into a narrow passageway. The hall led to a large iron hatch, which was bolted shut and secured with huge padlocks.

The same odd markings were carved into the edges of the entryway. Perhaps the scratches were meant to be a warning. Reagan held the dim flashlight closer to examine the symbols that now appeared to be some kind of celestial cryptograms.

When she ran her fingers over the etchings, the muttering amplified. Her body thrust forward against the door as if the souls were somehow reaching through solid steel, pulling her inside, syphoning the energy, the life from her. She wanted to scream, to escape, but the force held her breathless, immobile.

"Save my daddy." Destiny's cry resonated through the passageway, slicing the air, smothering the desperate wailing.

As quickly as the drone began, it ceased.

Reagan fell against the sidewall. Gasping for breath, she flew down the passageway and back up the stairs to the deck. She gripped her chest and darted past the giant mast. Driven by sheer panic, she ran toward the bow where she'd moored the pontoon--then halted.

"Destiny," she whispered. She couldn't just leave without doing a thorough search. Not after--

"Is someone there?" His muffled voice broke through the silence. "Please. Help me."

Reagan froze.

"Down here," he called out. "I'm down here."

Destiny's father? Perhaps. The child saw him fall near the towering mast. But the voice came from beneath her, below deck. Reagan had no interest in finding out what was in that hellhole beneath her. Passing the flashlight across the wooden planks, she perused the area for the source of the plea, but saw no one. Her flashlight flickered, dimming to little more than a soft glow. The batteries. Damn. Tiptoeing forward, she felt a crunch beneath her right shoe.

"Be careful," his voice warned. "The boards will collapse."

Without responding, Reagan lifted her foot and slowly drew it backward before pointing the light at the deck. Directly in front of her she saw more etchings similar to those that had been carved into other areas of the vessel, but this time the cryptograms were literally scorched into the floorboards of the deck. She was sure these marks were astrological in nature. She had seen them somewhere before, twelve unique symbols burned into a pie-shaped diagram.

The circle, about five feet in diameter, was charred so deeply in its center the boards disintegrated into ash. The slightest pressure would send them hurling downward, along with anything or anyone supplying the weight. A gaping hole edged with splintered burnt planks lay at the far side of the ring. The man below did not descend intentionally. The puzzle pieces fit. Des must have seen her father fall into the cryptic drawing.

"Are you alright?" Reagan directed her flashlight down the black hole, but the dim flicker's diminished glow had too little power to illuminate more than a shadowy image.

"I've been better." Relief flooded his voice. "I don't know where you came from Angel, but I'm sure as hell glad you're here."

"Don't count your blessings so fast." Reagan's cool reply reflected her skepticism. "Who are you?"

"Where are my manners? Introductions first, life saving later." He cleared his throat. "Monaco, ma'am. Jason Monaco. And to whom do I have the pleasure?"

"Sarcasm is probably not in your best interest under the circumstances." She strolled around the edge of the obscure design, inspecting it more closely. The symbols reminded her of something, but she couldn't put her finger on what. "I'm Reagan Nichols and, at the moment, your best way out of that pit."

"You're right, ma'am. My sincere apologizes."

"Accepted." She tested the floor then took a step forward and peered downward at Jason. "So. What's with this ship? And how did you manage to end up down there?"

"Beats me. When I saw this tub, my curiosity got the best of me." He chuckled. "Not one of my better decisions. Do you think you can find some rope or something?"

Reagan got down on her hands and knees before sprawling across the floor then she wriggled toward the huge hole. "Where are you, anyway?" She asked, shining the flashlight around the room below. The light sputtered, dimmed even more, barely enough for her to see his faint shadow turn to scan his surroundings.

"Hard to say." Jason replied, looking around the chamber. "Probably a cargo compartment of some kind. It's empty though."

"Hang on a sec." She scooted back, rolled to her side, then stood and brushed the soot off of her t-shirt and jeans. "I'm going to look around. There has to be something on this crate we can use to pull you up."

"Good plan." Jason yelled back. "I'll just hang out here and wait for you."

Reagan shook her head and rolled her eyes. "You're a real comedian."

After walking the entire length of the vessel, bow to stern, her frustration deepened. Every square inch of the rig was tied down or secured somehow and, despite the multitude of rope, she had no way of cutting it. The mast, though draped in ropes, provided nothing long enough to reach into the cargo area. But Reagan had always been resourceful. Determine your assets then improvise.

Jason called to her. "Any luck?"

"What are you wearing?" She edged closer to hole to assess his attire, but saw only a shadowy figure.

"Jeans and a polo shirt. Why?" he replied. "Am I underdressed?"

"Levity under stress...noted." She stepped back, walked over to the mast and fiddled with the rigging. "Take off your pants and shirt and throw them up to me, your belt too, if you have one."

"What, no foreplay?" He unhooked his belt and dropped his pants, took off his shirt, then tossed the clothing to Reagan.

Her smile would have given her tough-girl attitude away had Jason been able to see her face. "If you have any worthwhile suggestions, now would be a good time to mention them."

"I got nothin'."

She peered down at him. "I can see that," she lied. "Your lucky I found you."

"Yea, whatever possessed you to board this tub, anyway? It's not exactly inviting."

"Destiny." She tugged at the twine, twisting and weaving to extend the lengths.

"Des--"

"Don't worry, everything's cool. Right now let's just focus on getting you out of there."

"Right."

After manipulating the rigging with the brut force of her 110 pounds, Reagan finally managed to release enough rope to reach the cryptic imprint near the edge of the splintered planks.

"So, what were you doing lurking around my cove in the first place?" She slipped her own pants and t-shirt off, tied all the clothes together, stretching the fabric as much as possible.

"Your cove, huh? I didn't realize investigating National Park property was considered trespassing, Your Highness."

She dropped the clothing and her hands flew to her hips as she called down to him. "You really don't want to get out of there, do you, Mr. Monaco?"

"Sorry, Ms. Nichols. Again, my humble apologies." His figure bent over into a deep bow. "I was probing illegal chemical dumping in the lake."

"So are you some kind of detective?"

"No, an investigative journalist."

"Glad to know the lake's future is in the hands of such a competent man." She smirked.

Standing on the hem of his right jeans leg, she pulled each knot to tighten her handiwork. Using his belt to attach the string of clothes to the mast rigging, she fashioned a makeshift rope. "I hope you can reach this." She dropped it into the abyss. "I'm not strong enough to pull you up, but if you can shimmy high enough, I'll spread-eagle and reach down so you can grab my arms and climb out."

"Spread eagle, huh? Okay then." He tugged on the crude lanyard squeezing Reagan's fingers in the process.

"Ouch." She yanked her hand away and shook it back and forth. "Can you at least wait until I get in position?"

"Of course, Angel...It's crude...and may not hold long, but ingenious. This just might work."

"You doubted my ingenuity? Reagan stretched across the charred deck, knocking the flashlight into the cargo shaft. "Look out."

Jason ducked, his arms covering his head.

The light extinguished on impact.

"Perfect."

"Throwing things at me now, Angel?"

"Ahhh. Sorry. The batteries were about dead anyway." She dangled her arms into the chamber. "Okay, I'm ready when you are."

Yanking on the clothes again, he thrust upward to grab the highest point possible, then shimmied until he felt Reagan's hand. He gripped her wrists, leveraging her body to boost himself further so he could grab the crumbling, wooden deck. Reagan rolled to the side, pulling him with every once of her strength until his bare chest pressed against her face.

Without warning, the droning voices resumed, louder and louder until they echoed through the air. The vessel shuttered, rocking to and fro, thrashing the two around like rag dolls.

"What the hell?" Jason yelled over the clamor.

"Dear Lord, please...not again." Reagan clenched her eyes shut briefly and begged for the whine to stop.

Jason plunged forward, but the damaged floorboards gave way. His torso ripped across the splintered wood. To keep from falling, he clung to the first solid thing his hand could find--Reagan's shoulder--pinning her flat on her back.

Her left arm flailing, she grasped ahold of the clothing rope and slung it toward Jason. "Catch," she screamed.

The bulk of Jason's weight dangled between Reagan and a cracking plank. Releasing her, he grabbed the leg of his jeans and propelled himself toward the mast just as his shirt ripped from the rigging. He smashed onto the deck and rolled, with what was left of the clothing rope tangling around him. Reagan tumbled starboard then stood with her feet spread, trying to balance. Her upper body aching, she held out her hand to Jason.

"I got this." He dragged himself to his feet, draped the clothes around his neck. "For an angel, you sure have managed to piss off the devils."

"What makes you so sure it was me that riled them?"

The murmurs intensified, their metronomic whaling like the desperate outcry of a hundred lost souls tossing the sloop in nauseating rhythm.

"I'm pretty sure they don't like either of us, but this is no time to argue." He glanced around. "Now what? Any ideas how we get off this tub?"

"Come on, this way." Reagan grabbed Jason's hand and shot toward the bow where she moored her boat.

When they reached the railing a single beam of moonlight breached the fog like a beacon through ominous darkness. Jason grabbed the rigging and vaulted over the handrail, then balanced on the thin ledge. He held onto Reagan's wrist steadying her as she tried to mimic his actions.

The pontoon, though still tied to the ship, had drifted, thrust aside by the violent swaying of the larger vessel. Jason slid the clothes from his neck then crumpled and threw them into the pontoon. Then with the agility of a skilled gymnast, he clutched the rope, hoisted his legs outward, wrapped them around the thick twine and slid, hand over hand, down to the boat.

Paralyzed by the tumultuous water below, Reagan clung to the outside of the rail.

"You coming?" Holding the rope taut, Jason looked up at her with unwavering confidence. "Glide down, just like I did."

"I can't." She trembled, staring at the tossing pontoon through the swirling malevolent mist.

"You can do it, Reagan," he reassured her. "I've never met a woman with so much tenacity."

She looked over her shoulder, shuddering at the thought of the spirits sucking her into the chamber below, then turned and looked down at Jason. Grabbing the rope, she pushed forward off the ledge, but her injured rotator cuff weakened her grip. She couldn't lift her legs enough to wrap them around and secure her descent. She dangled, flinging back and forth with the tumultuous rhythm of the ship. Her hands burned as the rough twine sliced into her palms.

"Let go. I'll catch you." Jason stood below her, legs spread to maintain his balance, knees slightly bent, his arms held high ready to receive her.

She peered down in trepidation, hanging over the raging aquatic inferno, her palms stinging, slipping from her oozing blood.

"It's not that far. Just swing your body toward me." His conviction held firm. "I've got this, Angel. I promise I'll catch you."

The moonlight burst through the clouds and, for the first time, Reagan caught a glimpse of the man standing beneath her. The soft glow reflecting off the sea spray glistened on his bulging biceps and revealing a chiseled six-pack.

Propelling herself forward, Reagan released her grip and plunged. But Jason easily caught her. She slid down his moist body. Face to face, their eyes locked, and for a moment she felt lost in his moonlit gaze. His strong arms and warm skin drained her lingering fear.

The droning hum instantly ceased. The waters calmed. Startled by the abrupt silence, their trance broke and the two glanced around them.

"What do you say we blow this gig?" Jason chuckled.

"You untie the mooring, and I'll get the keys." Suddenly aware she was wearing nothing but her bra and panties, she turned to observe Jason, watching him as he bent over to unfasten the tether, his fitted boxers leaving little to her imagination. The corners of her mouth curled upward. Des's dad was quite a hunk--"Oh my gosh, Des," she whispered, then called to Jason. "Can we take off?"

"We're good." He tossed the mooring aside.

Turning the ignition, Reagan tried to determine how long she'd been gone. Two hours at the most. She assured Jason his daughter was fine when she first found him. No need to worry him now, not after all they had been through. Hopefully Des was still tucked into Reagan's bed fast asleep. Deep in thought, she gazed up to see Jason standing beside her.

"It's over Angel." He placed his warm hands on her shoulders and began to massage her neck. "I'm not sure what the hell just happened, but we're safe now."

The ebony sky lightened as they navigated closer to shore. Moonlight broke through the shadows with their forward motion, casting a soft glow across the wake. But the ship, masked by its murky veil loomed behind them, still shrouded in malevolence.

Reagan reached up and stroked Jason's arm. "I hope so."

She'd always been levelheaded. Supernatural forces occurred only in science fiction, not the real world. But after tonight she knew otherwise. She was confident that whatever brought the vessel to her cove possessed dark intentions. How they eluded the grip of pure evil escaped her, but she had no doubt they were well within its grasp.

She pulled up beside her dock, relieved to be back home. Jason hopped off the pontoon and, rope in hand, pulled the boat close to secure the craft to the cleats.

Looking around, he stared at the vague image of the cabin through the trees. "Not to sound cliché, but what's a nice girl like you doing in a place like this? Living alone so far from society? You hiding from someone?"

"I think myself more than anyone else." After what they just experienced, running away from her family to sulk like a petulant child now seemed petty and insignificant. She had wonderful parents, a sister who loved her--and she loved them with all her heart. Why did she react to her adoption so irrationally? Her family must be frantic about her whereabouts.

"Trying to find yourself, huh?" He offered a wry grin. "How's that working for you?"

"Well, until this evening, not so great." Grabbing the keys, she stepped onto the dock, looked at her underwear, then back at Jason.

Sensing her embarrassment, he smiled. "Yeah, I usually don't show up for a first date dressed like this either." He eyed her up and down. "But there are no complaints here." He leaned over, grabbed their clothes and tossed them to Reagan.

She raised an eyebrow, pursed her lips and eyed him, yanking at the knot that held her wife-beater to Jason's jeans. When the tie released, she pitched his pants at him, then slipped into her jeans and tee. Her eyes drifted to him, his skin glistening in the moonlight as he zipped up and buckled his pants caused a warm tingle to surge through her.

She turned toward the cabin to avoid exposing the visceral responses she felt just looking at his muscular body. "Come on," she said over her shoulder. "I can't wait to see Des's face when she sees you."

"Des?" His puzzled tone begged a response.

"Sorry. Just a nickname I concocted." She glanced at Jason, then back at the path. "I mean Destiny."

"Destiny," he echoed.

"She's an amazing child," Reagan added. "If it weren't for her, you'd still be wandering around in that pit."

Jason paused at the foot of the steps. "I'm sorry, but I'm completely confused. I assume Destiny is your daughter, but what did she have to do with you finding me in the cargo hold of that hellhole of a ship?"

Reagan stopped cold. She grabbed his arm and stared at him, her wrinkled brow showing complete bewilderment. "Des isn't your daughter?"

"I don't have a daughter." He rubbed the stubbles on his chin then smirked. "At least not one I know of."

"If you're not her father, who is the little girl sleeping in my room?" Reagan could feel the blood drain from her face. Maybe Jason wasn't the only man stranded on that vessel. She couldn't bear the thought of having to go back to look for the little girl's father.

"I found Destiny around dusk, wandering through the woods. She kept insisting I save her daddy from that ship. When I found you, I just assumed--" Reagan trembled, peered over her shoulder toward the mist hovering over the ghostly craft and held onto Jason's chest.

"Hold on. Take a deep breath, Reagan." He placed his hands around her waist. "Why don't we go inside and talk to her. If her dad is still out there, we'll call the cops and get some help to get him off that tub." He pulled her closer. "There's no way I'm letting you get anywhere near that tank again."

Reagan squeezed his hand. "I have to make sure she is alright." She tore up the steps, threw open the screen door and ran straight into the bedroom with Jason following close behind.

Staring at her empty bed, she called out in alarm, "Destiny."

Jason placed his palms on her arms, turned her around and glared into her eyes. "Calm down, Angel. We'll find her."

Reagan crumpled her brow. "Something's not right." She pulled away, scurried through the great room into the kitchen, taking note of every detail.

The damp towel she used to wipe Des's hands and face before tossing it next to the sink, hung neatly on the cabinet hook. The empty bowl of macaroni and the plate of sliced strawberries no longer sat on the counter. Reagan's eyes drifted to the bottle of vodka next to the sink. The seal hadn't been broken. No graham crackers or empty hot chocolate cups lingered on the coffee table, no chocolate bars or marshmallows. Reagan glanced at the front door where she'd meticulously placed Des's tiny white paten-leather shoes-- they had vanished.

"You okay, Reagan?"

She felt the concern in his voice. The truth was Reagan hadn't felt okay since twilight fell and that murky mist oozed inland. And where was Des? Had she imagined the child-- fantasized the whole incident?

Reagan ambled back toward the bedroom, pausing in front of Jason. "I honestly don't know."

Gazing around him, she stared blankly at her untouched bed. The comforter lay folded neatly at the foot where she positioned the blanket every morning since she'd arrived at the cabin. Her pillows, fluffed and set at an angle, rested precisely the way she routinely arranged them. Not a single trace of evidence that Destiny had ever existed lingered anywhere.

Jason drew her close, hugging her in an affectionate embrace. "We'll find her, Reagan. I promise."

"You don't understand." Reagan collapsed into him. "She's not just gone. It's as if she was never here." She pulled back slightly, wrapped her arms around his neck and laid her head against his warm chest. "I'm not crazy. I swear I'm not. I didn't imagine her."

"I believe you, Reagan." He smoothed a strand of hair from her eyes and tucked it behind her left ear. "No one would believe what happened on that ship tonight. Hell, they'd think we were crazy if we said a ship drifted into Spirit Lake at all. But we know the truth." He ran his finger across her cheek. "Something supernatural has happened here--to both of us. You would never have found me if it hadn't been for that little girl. It doesn't matter where she came from or where she went. No one will ever convince me she didn't exist.

"Then you don't think I'm a raving lunatic?"

"He lifted her chin with the crook of his forefinger. "If you are, I'm right there with you."

Reagan gazed up and stared into his deep violet eyes. She could finally see Jason, his tousled sandy brown hair highlighted with golden strands, his chiseled features and full luscious lips. An intense wave of primitive passion, the likes of which she'd never felt, surged through her.

He leaned into her, pressing his bare chest against hers, slid his hand behind her neck and, gently grasping her hair, tilted her head back. When his lips touched hers, Reagan closed her eyes and melted into him.

§

High above Hidden Cove Destiny giggled as she watched her parents kiss.

"You did well, little one." Michael placed his hand on her shoulder and smiled, the soft glow of the harvest moon shimmering through their evanescent images.

Ghosts and spirits loom dark and foreboding across this world, lurking in obscure shadows, swirling amidst murky mist, or concealed within the dusty corners of tortured minds twisting dreams into nightmares. The struggle between good and evil endures eternal, especially at Spirit Lake where myriad lost souls wander the shores and slumber beneath the surface. Apparitions linger throughout the hollow biding time in transition, souls of the dead––but also souls of those yet to be born.

Destiny tugged on Michael's robe. "When can I hug my mommy again? And I so want to meet my daddy."

"Soon my child, very soon. You're bravery has made it so." Turning, he peered downward at the nefarious ship and with a soft puff of his angelic breath, the fog-cloaked vessel vanished into the haunting mist. Michael smiled at Destiny, draped one arm around the child's shoulder and waved his other hand high above their heads in a circular motion. They swirled together into a blaze of lavender light that streaked over the lake, swallowing the mysterious haze before bursting into a blanket of stars across the midnight sky.

The Gift

Book Two

Casi McLean

The Gift

She didn't plan to leave. It was a knee-jerk reaction. Savannah's emotions erupted like spewing lava. She had to escape––to think. She'd call Ryan to explain when she got to the lake, after she pulled herself together.

Savy tucked her long, bronze hair behind one ear and glanced into the rearview mirror. Delicate snowflakes drifted on the cold December air, simple, beautiful. At the moment she longed for simplicity. How did her life suddenly get so complicated? Yesterday her world ran like a fine tuned clock. She worked hard to break into the inner circle of the fashion community and made a name for herself despite Ramon, her temperamental boss. Why did her life have to turn upside-down now?

The familiar tune I'll Be There chimed on her smartphone. Ryan. Savy gazed at his smiling face, hesitated, then touched ignore. The song immediately stopped, the picture disappeared. She couldn't talk to him. Not yet. Taking off without a word was so un-Savy-like. She didn't want to worry him. Ryan Patterson meant everything to her. She truly loved him. His mere presence stirred her deepest desires. But the situation warranted more than passion, didn't it?

From the very first moment she met Ryan, everything between them flowed like water. No drama, no compromise, their relationship was easy. They fit together like puzzle pieces. Ryan treated her like a princess, an uncommon attribute these days, or so she thought. He supported her career, encouraged her to leave Ramon's Designs and start her own company. That was her plan. Her life made sense and her relationship worked––that is until this morning.

Savy wasn't sure if Ramon felt threatened by her, believed in her, or just wanted to get rid of her, but the reasoning didn't matter. Living in London for a year submerged in the fashion capital of the world surpassed her wildest dreams. Maybe she could even mingle with Kate Middleton. Turning down an opportunity like this would be a total and complete professional blunder, wouldn't it?

Silent snow fell harder now, blanketing the countryside, dusting the road as she drove north. Flurries that floated on the air in Atlanta now swirled around her in a crystalline wonderland. The night would have been perfect, sharing a snowy Christmas Eve with the love of her life, a roaring fire, a soft merlot and candlelight kisses.

Visceral responses washed over her at the thought, intensified by the romantic Martin Nievera melody--until she realized the source of the music, Ryan calling again. She grabbed her phone from the console and stared at his sensuous smile, her finger hovering over the accept button. When the call transferred to voice mail she turned the sound off and placed her cell back in its cubby, while her thoughts drifted to their last conversations.

"I really wanted to plan something special for you, Savy. Our first Christmas together should be memorable."

"A candlelight dinner at your place will be perfect." She smiled envisioning an amorous evening. "Can I bring anything? Wine, or an appetizer, cheese, grapes?"

"I've taken care of everything. I should be home by five, but if I'm not there when you arrive, just use your key." He cleared his throat to emphasize his reminder. "That's what it's for you know."

"I know. Bear with me," she teased. "I'm still getting used to the idea."

"Right. I've got to run, beautiful. See you at five." He paused for a moment then added, "I love you Savannah Emily Bradford."

"I love you too, babe. See you tonight."

Savy arrived a five pm on the dot. When Ryan didn't answer the doorbell, she pulled out her new key and tentatively let herself in. His condo was always immaculate, another endearing quality, but tonight the ambiance overwhelmed her. The place practically glistened. When she entered, the two-story foyer greeted her with a seven-foot Christmas tree set into the curve of the spiral staircase. The flocked tree, perfectly decorated with Victorian ornaments, was exactly as she had described to Ryan in her dream-Christmas.

She placed the gifts she brought for him on the skirt then strolled into the great room. Ryan had set a beautiful table in front of the fireplace with candles, wine, linen napkins, and a centerpiece boasting an elaborate display of gardenias intermingled with deep red roses––Savy's favorites. The soft scent floated through his entire condo.

Savannah breathed in deeply. She felt cherished just knowing that Ryan cared enough to listen when she told him little details, her likes and dislikes. The whole setting looked as if he transported her dreams. Perfection catered by an elegant upscale restaurant and designed just for her. She took off her coat and hung it in the closet. Her phone rang as she closed the door.

"Sorry, babe." Ryan's tone was tinged with frustration. "I'm not sure if it's Christmas or the snow, but traffic is crazy downtown."

"That's fine. Take your time." She assured him. "I have to admit, I'm really impressed, Ryan. The decorations look beautiful, and the table..."

"I'm glad you like my surprise so far. I'll be there as soon as I can, sweetie. Just make yourself at home."

When she hung up the phone, Savy poured herself a glass of wine, connected her cell to the docking station and played some romantic music before wandering into the kitchen to see what Ryan prepared for dinner. Glancing into the laundry room on her way to the fridge, she noticed a pile of clean clothes on top of the washer. On impulse, she set her wine on the table, folded the garments then carried them into the bedroom to put them away.

It wasn't until she opened the closet to hang Ryan's shirts that her curiosity got the best of her. A bright red Christmas bag caught her eye. Like a six-year-old, she grabbed the bag to peek inside. That's when she saw it.

There was no disguising the turquoise-blue Tiffany & Co. bag. Her heart pounding, she reached inside and pulled out a tiny turquoise box. When she opened it, a lump knotted in her throat and she couldn't breathe. Among Ryan's Christmas gifts in that little turquoise box was the most spectacular engagement ring she'd ever seen.

Savy's thoughts hurtled into panic mode. She loved Ryan with all her heart, but marriage...now...what about London? Her big surprise was to tell him all about her big promotion, which included a year in the fashion capitol of the world.

She wanted...she needed to talk to him and tell him about her incredible career opportunity, but now...how could she even broach the subject. She couldn't. Not after what she found in his closet.

If Ryan hadn't been running late, they would have shared a beautiful romantic evening together while Savannah remained in blissful ignorance of his intentions, and still floating on air over her job––or maybe not.

Perhaps he planned to give her the ring that night. After all, it was Christmas Eve, the perfect moment to--she would have been blind-sided. So instead, Savy acted on impulse again. She replaced the gift in its hiding place, grabbed her coat and phone, then left. No note. No warning. She simply got in her Acura and headed toward the solace of her little RV at the lake.

§

On an ordinary night, Savy could drive to her property with rote precision, but not tonight. Scant vehicles, few and far between, left tracks in the snow signposting the twists and turns of the narrow highway beneath a frosty white blanket. Snowflakes spun swirling endlessly to-and-fro, reflecting off her headlights.

She gripped the steering wheel tighter and glared through the icy windshield, hoping to see between each swish-swish of the wipers. The tracks ahead skidded off to the right, but by the time she saw them her car slid sideways. An ice patch, smooth and deadly jettisoned her steering. She slammed on the brakes. But instead of responding, the Acura slid with inertia toward an embankment until her tires made contact with hard-packed snow. Turning into the slide, she regained some semblance of control before the mound clenched her tires and stifled her momentum.

What was she thinking driving up to the lake in the first place? Not a difficult question to answer. The lure of the lake, the solace and solitude, held mystical tranquility for Savy, a place where she could decompress, think and create.

She loved her property, a tract so close to the mountains she could smell the clean air. The view was spectacular, but she never considered navigating the curvy roads on a snowy evening. The wind whistled, shifting her car, luring it toward more mounding drifts along the roadside. Ice crawled across trees limbs pressing branches together into a mesmeric maze.

Driving on the highway through the snowstorm challenged her enough, but the side roads, buried beneath a blanket of snow, were completely obscured. Once off the beaten trail, she had only her instincts and the space between snow-laden trees to mark the road ahead.

She inched forward. If she could only see a landmark she'd know where she was. She knew the area so well, she had memorized every inch of her land from the hand carved tree-trunk mailbox she planted the day she bought her property, to the curve of the lake at the water's edge. But soft snow carpeted everything in sight. There were no landmarks to be seen; everywhere she gazed she saw a never-ending crystalline wonderland.

Aside from the muted music from her satellite radio, the only sound that broke the silence was the purr of her engine. Who else would be crazy enough to be out on a night like this, especially on Christmas Eve? Most people were home with loved ones, but not Savannah Bradford.

Visions of Ryan, alone and completely confused, tormented her. He didn't deserve what she did. Leaving like that was insolent, inconsiderate and he had to be worried sick. Savy stopped the car. She had simply freaked out. When she picked up her cell phone to call Ryan, the entire screen glowed with his missed calls. She pressed the screen to return his call. She had to reach him, tell him what had happened and why she tore off in a panic.

There was no easy way to choose between Ryan and London. But maybe she wouldn't have to choose. He knew how important her career was to her, how hard she worked to be recognized in the industry. He would understand.

Of course he couldn't just ditch his own career and go with her, but the year would sail by quickly. And with today's technology, she could see him on Face Time and text every day. Besides, he would only be a flight away. Their romance didn't have to end just because she had a gig in London.

Savy touched her phone screen again and again. The impulse sent but the call failed. No service. Perfect. The least she could do was pick up his messages and head home. She'd try him again on her way back to Atlanta.

Scrolling to her voicemail, she listened to Ryan's frantic messages, berating herself for her impetuous behavior.

"Sav, where are you? You poured yourself a glass of wine and left?" His voice showed clear confusion. "Did something happen? Call me."

The phone beeped to the next message.

"I'm getting a little concerned. Please call me, sweetie." Beep...

"Savy, you're starting to worry me. Let me know what's up." Beep...

"Savy, where the hell are you? It's snowing like crazy out there. I'm worried about you." Beep...

"Savannah please babe, let me know what's going on." Beep...

"If I don't hear from you soon...Sav...this isn't like you. What happened?" Beep...

"I love you sweetheart. Please, call me when you can." The messages stopped.

"Oh my gosh, Ryan. I'm so sorry," Savannah apologized out loud. She started the engine again, threw her car into gear and spun her steering wheel. But turning around in the snow wasn't easy. Thank God she invested in decent all-weather tires. The last thing she needed was to be stranded out in the middle of nowhere. She'd probably freeze to death. They'd discover her ice-covered, blue body days from now crouched into a fetal position with an expression of sheer panic frozen on her face.

She shivered at the thought. "Okay, Sav. Cut the drama and get the hell out of this dismal place." She backed up again then shifted into drive and pressed the accelerator. Her tires spun, slipping on a coat of sheer ice. "No . . ." She screamed at her Acura as if her voice would somehow jolt the car forward. "This can't be happening."

Remembering how her father rocked the car back and forth to grab traction, she threw the gears into reverse, then back into drive over-and-over until the car finally moved, but instead of pulling forward, it surged backwards until her rear passenger-side tire plunged into a ditch.

§

Completely wedged into the trench, Savy weighed her options. She wouldn't freeze to death trying to stay warm in an Acura tomb.

The vivid image still fresh in her mind, she glanced around for an alternative solution. The snow had stopped, only a light flurry lingered floating on the wind and the moon shown brightly through crystal-glazed trees. A narrow road, or a trail of some kind, twisted around the forest and beyond where a distant light glimmered.

Savy, with her cashmere coat covering the slinky red silk dress she designed herself, had worn three-inch heels. Where were her boots when she needed them? She pushed the door open, stepped out into a snowdrift and sunk knee-deep into the ditch. Clomping through ice-packed snow in little more than bare feet, she finally made her way across the clearing to the winding path. Her toes frozen and numb to the bone, she trudged toward a beacon, a lighthouse gleaming amidst a snowy fantasyland.

As she approached, she could see that the brilliant glow was nothing more than a miniature Christmas tree, set on the window seat of a quaint cottage snuggled into the woods. Yes...a home, warmth, and perhaps a landline so she could call Ryan.

Shivering, she teetered toward the front door, slipping only occasionally on the icy driveway. A lovely wrap-around porch stretched around the house. And a lone, worn wooden rocking chair, glazed in ice, swayed to-and-fro in the wind. As forlorn as it appeared, Savy had to fight the urge to sit down and test its comfort. She rapped on the door, waited a few minutes before knocking again. The knob turned and the oak door cracked open.

"Why child." And elderly woman with sparkling blue eyes and long white hair twisted into a French braid peered around the door. "What in the world are you doing dressed like that out in this cold ...and on Christmas Eve?"

"I'm so sorry to bother you, Ma'am." Shivering, Savy tucked her hair behind her ears. "But my car is stuck in a ditch up the road a ways and I have no phone service. I was wondering if you had a landline I could use?"

"Come in, child." The old woman opened the door and stood back to let Savy enter. "Come in. You must be freezing."

"Thank you Ma'am--"

"Emma, dear. Please call me Emma."

"Thank you, Emma." Savy stepped inside. "It is a bit chilly out there."

"Come and warm yourself by the fire, child." She motioned toward a huge hearth with a roaring blaze. "Would you like a cup of tea? I was just making some for myself."

"That would be lovely, Ma'am"--the woman held up her hand in protest, stopping Savy mid-sentence--"I mean Emma. Do you have a phone I could use?"

"I'm sorry, dear. I'm afraid the storm got to it first. But you're welcome to stay until you can haul your car out." She scurried toward a hallway that presumably led to the kitchen. "Tea will be ready in a few minutes. The water is already boiling. Please, make yourself at home, child."

"It's Savannah. Savannah Bradford."

Emma halted, turned and stared at Savy with a peculiar expression. After an awkward silent moment, she spoke. "Savannah. What an exquisite name." She turned back toward the kitchen and wobbled out of sight.

Emma's weird hesitation sent a wave of anxiety slithering down Savy's spine. She had no idea who this woman was. The old lady could have been an ax-murderer for all Savy knew.

Her creative juices pumping, she imagined Emma a homicidal maniac in the guise of a little old lady, who lured her prey into her quaint little cottage only to offer up a cup of homemade arsenic tea. Perhaps Savy had chosen the wrong career. A frustrated writer lurked in her soul. She giggled and shook off her trepidation.

Savy wandered around the living room inspecting the knickknacks Emma had accumulated over the years. Souvenirs from countries all over the world adorned her tables and mantle. Her furniture was of the finest quality with hand woven fabrics and classic period pieces. The woman clearly had traveled extensively and must have been quite successful in her day.

Savy strolled over to the Christmas tree that had beckoned her from the distance. It was small, artificial but made of a material Savy hadn't seen before. The needles looked so real and they smelled of pine with fine flocking that didn't rub off when she touched it. Probably European. They had the most beautiful craftsmanship across the pond. Savy loved the little tree with its detailed Victorian ornaments and sparkling lights, exactly what she would have chosen herself.

"Pretty little thing, isn't it?" Emma ambled into the room with a tray sporting a beautiful china teapot, an assortment of fine English tea and warm crumpets.

What a timely treat. Perhaps it was a sign that choosing London was in the cards. Savy smiled. "Have you ever been to England, Emma?"

She placed the tray on the coffee table. "I spent a good portion of my life in London." She poured water from the pot into a cup and handed it to Savy. " And you?"

"I haven't been there yet. But I'm planning a trip." Savy dipped an Earl Grey teabag into the steamy water, chose a crumpet drizzled with chocolate icing then leaned back into her wingback chair. "I leave right after New Years and will be there for a year." She grinned.

"A year is a long time, dear." Emma poured her own cup and sat down. "Won't your family and friends miss you?"

"I suppose." She blew on the hot tea before taking a sip. "But it's such a wonderful opportunity to advance my career."

"Oh? What kind of work do you do?" Emma raised an eyebrow, then pulled the hot brew to her nose and breathed in the aroma.

Despite the woman's odd reclusive nature, Savy couldn't help but be drawn to her. She was kind and had a wisdom about her that Sav admired. The two women chatted about cabbages and kings for an hour or so before she noticed that Emma displayed no pictures in the room.

No frames cramped together on the mantle, no albums lining bookshelves or handmade treasures tucked between family heirlooms. How odd for an elderly woman to have no signs of her family. Surely she'd want to boast about her children and grandchildren.

"It must be lonely living so isolated way out here. Does your family live close by?"

"No, child." Emma shifted in her chair. "That's the biggest regret of my life."

"Regret?" Savy's tone begged elaboration. "But you have traveled the world and have a lovely home. You must have been quite successful in your day."

"Success? Perhaps." Emma set her cup on the coffee table. "But as beauty is in the eyes of the beholder, success fragments the hearts of fools."

A strange choice of words, Savy wasn't sure she even understood the comment and her puzzled look gave her away.

"There is no family, dear one. My parents passed when I was a child and I have no living relatives. No precious pictures to place on my mantle or memories to hold in my heart." Emma leaned back against the soft pillows lining her sofa. "I married my career, Savannah. There was no time for love. No husband to come home to or children to cherish. I loved my work so much I pushed everything else out of my life."

"But you had a lifetime of memories, right?" Savy pointed her chin toward the mantle. "Just look at all your trophies and souvenirs."

"Awards and titles won't keep you warm at night, laugh with you, or comfort you. It's a lonely road to traverse." Emma reached over and placed her hand on Savy's as she reached for the last crumpet. "It's the people in life that matter, Savy, not the things." She pulled her hand away and smiled. "Don't squander your chance for true love like I did, child. London will be there tomorrow, but love will not."

Emma stood and strolled over to the little Christmas tree. "You know, I've had this tree for fifty years, but there has never been a single gift beneath it." She softly stroked an ornament, a crystal angel with wings twisted into a heart. The intricate detail caught the light on every angle creating a dazzling effect that seemed to emanate from within.

"What a beautiful piece." Savy stood and approached Emma, staring at the decoration as she walked toward the tree.

"She was a gift from the man I should have married." Emma turned to Savy. "He told me that she gleams from within with the power of love." Emma smiled, touched Savy on the shoulder. "You must be exhausted, child. My guest room has fresh sheets and there are towels in the linen closet. Please, I'd be honored if you'd be my guest this Christmas Eve. It would warm my heart to have you here."

Of course Savy had nowhere else to stay or the ability to leave, but she felt compassion for the lonely old woman and wanted Emma to have someone with whom to share her Christmas morning. "How thoughtful of you. Thank you for your gracious hospitality."

Emma picked up the tray and headed toward the kitchen. "The guest room is the first at the top of the stairs. I hope you like it. The balcony overlooks the lake."

"I'm sure the room is lovely." Savy moved toward the stairs. "I am drained though." She mounted the steps and dragged her weary body upward. The day had been an emotional roller coaster and she welcomed a restful sleep.

Flashing on Ryan, she rebuked herself again and prayed he would be able to rest through the night. She had not only ruined their Christmas Eve, she'd pulled through hell the most amazing man she'd ever known. But tomorrow morning she would dig her car out of the ditch and drive back to Atlanta. She'd explain what happened and he'd understand. He had to.

After a soothing hot shower, Savy wrapped herself in a fluffy cotton towel, padded back to her room and collapsed on the bed, sinking into a mattress the likes of which she had never felt before. Beyond comfortable, the foam cushion lulled her into a sorely needed slumber, while Emma's warning whispered through her mind: "It's the people in life that matter, Savy, not the things."

When dawn broke through the midnight sky, Savy awoke with sensuous thoughts of Ryan. His sensuous features, dark brown hair, deep green eyes and seductive smile aroused the woman inside of her. Stretching, she opened her eyes and gazed across the bedroom to the terrace and the wintery fairyland surrounding the lake. The breathtaking view glistened in the morning sunlight.

After straightening her bed, she slipped back into her red silk dress, picked up her heels, then padded downstairs. Emma, already awake, had baked fresh croissants. Creamery butter and honey sat on the kitchen table next to a steaming teapot and a box of Earl Grey tea.

"Merry Christmas, Savannah." The old woman grinned from ear to ear.

"Merry Christmas." She put her high heel shoes next to the door.

Emma sat at the table. "Won't you join me for breakfast?"

Savy preferred eating light in the morning and a freshly baked croissant with tea was her breakfast of choice. Of course Emma had no way of knowing that. "It's perfect," Savy said in earnest.

After their meal, Savy stood. "As wonderful as it has been to meet you, Emma, I have to dig my car out and get back to Atlanta. Ryan must be frantic with worry."

"Your young man, yes dear, it's Christmas. You should skedaddle." Emma's mouth curled into a deep grin. "But I have something to give you before you leave." She stood and toddled toward the living room. "Come, child. You don't want to waste any time getting back to that man of yours."

Savy placed her dishes into the sink, picked up her shoes then joined Emma in the living room, where she stood next to her little Christmas tree.

"You see?" Emma's eyes lit up as she shifted them to a beautifully wrapped present under the tree. "Finally, a gift beneath my tree." She reached over, picked up the box and handed it to Savy. "It's for you, dear one."

"A gift? For me?" Savy's puzzled gaze scrunched her face. "It is I who should be giving you a present for taking me in last night."

"You have given me a gift far greater than you know, dear." Emma smiled. "Don't open it now, child. There will be plenty of time to open gifts once you are back home with your young man." She reached in the closet, pulled out Savy's coat and gave it to her. "Let's get you on the road, Savannah."

"Thank you so much for everything." Savy stuffed the gift into her coat pocket, pulled her heels on then turned and hugged Emma. "I have a home close by...well, right now it's just a little RV but I plan to build on the lot one day. I'd love to have you come by sometime."

"You can rely on that, dear." Emma smiled. "Now hurry on."

Savy waved to Emma as she walked away, promising to return soon with directions to her property--once she figured out exactly where it was from here. When she approached her car in the light of day, she could see her predicament more clearly. The snow had melted a little already, typical of north Georgia weather. It could be thirty degrees and snowing one day and a sunny sixty the next.

Savy opened the door, reached into the console for her keys, then took off her coat and slid inside. She put her wrap on the passenger seat and turned the ignition. The car, wedged into a ditch, could move forward if she straightened her wheels and rocked back-and-forth again. She did so, spinning slush and mud all over.

Traction. She needed something to create traction beneath her tires. Remembering the cardboard boxes she had gotten with her groceries at Costco, she popped the trunk then tottered around to the back of the car. When she saw her workout bag, she rolled her eyes. Running shoes, yoga pants and a sweatshirt would have been much more appropriate attire in the snow than a slinky dress and heels.

Oh well, better late than never. She shrugged, leaned against the bumper and attempted to change her shoes, but in the process, she slipped and fell smack dab into an old stump that lay conspicuously close to the side of the road.

§

Pulling herself to her feet, Savy reached for the towel in her gym bag then wiped the slush from her face and dress. She turned to toss the towel into her trunk and caught a glimpse of some letters carved into the stump. When she brushed the snow away--she froze.

There, carved into the front of the mailbox the name Savannah Emily Bradford glared back at her. Completely baffled, she wiped more snow from the hand-carved stump and stared back toward the cottage. Savy turned in every direction but saw no one, nothing but the snow-dusted landscape. She stripped, dressed in her workout garb, then hurried back toward the cottage and Emma.

Rounding the bend in the road, she halted. Emma's home no longer caressed the shoreline. Instead, a small RV parked at angle faced the lake--Savy's RV. It made no sense...Emma's house was there only moments ago. Savy shook her head.

She hadn't imagined the cottage, or the old woman. The whole evening was vividly real. Savy darted toward her makeshift lake home, flew up the steps and burst through the door. Everything in sight appeared to be exactly as she had left it.

Collapsing on her bed, she stared at the ceiling. Had her entire Christmas Eve been a dream or some psychotic hallucination? Maybe the exhaust fumes seeped to her brain. Oddly though, whatever happened to Savy in the last twelve hours changed her perspective. Flashing on Emma, Savannah bolted up with a jolt.

"She called me Savy." Emma had called her child, dear one, and Savannah throughout the evening, but in the one comment seared in Savy's mind, she was sure Emma had used her nickname.

"It's the people in life that matter, Savy, not the things," Emma said. "Don't squander your chance for true love like I did, child. London will be there tomorrow, but love will not."

How did Emma know to call her Savy? It was not a common nickname. Perhaps the evening was nothing but a bizarre dream conjured from the corners of Savannah's mind.

Regardless, Emma helped Savy make the most important decision of her life. She didn't want to end up sad and alone like the frail, elderly woman. Savy would start her own fashion design company like she planned. London would always be there if she had the desire to visit, but she wouldn't leave Ryan behind.

"Ryan," she whispered aloud. She had to go home and tell him what happened. And if she were still lucky enough to have him ask her to marry him, she would fly into his arms with an emphatic yes.

Savy rushed back to her car, pulled the cardboard boxes from the trunk and shoved them under her tires. When she started the ignition and shifted into drive, the car easily pulled back onto the slushy road. Grabbing her smartphone, she tried to call Ryan, but the service remained down. When she got closer to Atlanta, she'd try again. In the mean time, she needed to focus on driving home.

§

Ryan was frantic with worry. When Savannah drove up, he was waiting outside, arms held out to hug her before she stepped out of the car. She slung her purse over her shoulder, grabbed her phone and threw open the door.

"Oh Ryan. I'm so sorry I left like that and worried you so." Tears streamed down her cheeks. "Please forgive me."

He lifted Savy off her feet and swung her around. "I'm just glad you're alright, sweetie." He loosened his grip, letting her slide down his chest to her feet. Then he reached his hand beneath her long bronze locks, tilted her head backward and pressed his mouth over hers. After a long passionate embrace, he pulled back and gazed into her eyes. "I love you Savannah Emily Bradford...but please, don't ever scare me like that again."

"I promise." She looked at him through her eyelashes. "I don't know what I was thinking."

After grabbing her coat from the car, Ryan grasped Savy's hand in his and headed inside. "You do owe me an explanation though." He raised an eyebrow.

"Yes, I do." She smiled and cocked her head. "But I'm not sure you are going to believe me."

Ryan's condo was even more beautiful in the light of day and the table hadn't been touched, save the missing bottle of merlot. The amazing Christmas tree he tastefully decorated just for Savy glittered with sparkling lights and dazzling ornaments. Beneath the tree mingled with the presents she had brought the night before were three new gifts, all addressed to Savy.

"You hungry?" Ryan took her hand, led her toward the table in front of the fireplace.

"Famished." She didn't dare tell him she had stuffed herself with croissants a few hours earlier. She disappointed him once. That wouldn't happen again--at least not intentionally.

"Good." He offered a wry smile. "It seems I have a gourmet meal just waiting for you." He pulled out the chair for her then, turning the fire down to a soft glow, grabbed a pitcher and poured orange juice into her champagne glass. "It's a little early for wine, but I thought mimosa's would be in order."

"Perfect," she replied in earnest.

After a delectable catered meal fit for a queen, Ryan led Savy to the beautiful flocked tree.

"Merry Christmas, Sav." He kissed her cheek then kneeled to pick up a gift. "Open this one first." He handed the small box to Savy.

Her heart pounded inside her chest as she pulled off the bow and peeled back the paper. Reaching beneath the tissue, she drew out a sparkling crystal angel with wings that melted around her and twisted into a heart.

"Oh my gosh." She held the glittering ornament up. The lights from the tree glistened as they refracted off the diamond cuts of the crystal.

Ryan grinned at Savy's astonished reaction. "She gleams from within with the power of love." He kissed her forehead.

Savy stared at the image then into Ryan's deep green eyes. "Where did you get this?"

"I saw her on my last trip to Ireland and had to buy her for you." He smiled a grin of pure satisfaction.

"She's...amazing." Stunned, Savy remembered Emma's comment about her own crystal angel. "She was a gift from the man I should have married. He told me she gleams from within with the power of love."

"I'm so glad you like her."

Savannah choked back her astonishment until she could find the words to explain to Ryan her mystical encounter with Emma.

"That's quite a coincidence. The guy had excellent taste." He chuckled and bent down to pick up another gift.

"Wait." She touched his shoulder. "It's my turn."

Her gifts to Ryan seemed meager now, despite having labored over her choices for weeks. An Italian leather wallet, an espresso/latte machine and a set of Copenhagen glasses sure to please the most distinguished man. Yet they paled in comparison to Ryan's gift to her. He unwrapped each present with an expression of genuine gratitude.

When he handed Savy the last gift from beneath the tree, her heart sunk. The large box couldn't be an engagement ring, which meant her entire tirade was a self-induced freak-out. And now, she wanted to marry Ryan more than anything else in the world.

She pulled off the glittering silver bow, carefully unwrapped each corner of the shinny platinum paper and opened the box. Inside, underneath some white tissue paper was another box. It was smaller, but wrapped with the same paper and precision.

Within each box was another and another until the final gift was only two inches in diameter, the size of the ring box she'd seen in Ryan's closet the night before. Her heart raced.

She looked at Ryan, heat flushing over her face, she found herself pleading to find the Tiffany ring inside the final container.

"Are you going to open that thing, or stare at it all day?" Ryan teased.

Savy slowly peeled the paper back to reveal the familiar turquoise box.

As she opened it, Ryan took her hand and fell to his knees.

"I love you, Savannah Emily Bradford." He cleared his throat and quivered. "Will you marry me?"

"Yes," she replied without hesitation, then chortled. "Oh yes."

He stood, pulled the beautiful ring from its case and placed it on her finger.

The embrace that followed drew passion from Savy she didn't know she had. For the next several hours they played, teasing each other, enticing their innermost desires. Savy knew she made the right choice. She couldn't have been more sure of her decision had she pondered over it for years.

When the evening sky drenched the horizon in a pink and purple haze, Ryan finally probed Savy for an explanation to clarify her eccentric behavior on Christmas Eve. She divulged the entire story, including Emma's comment about the angel, leaving only a few details unturned.

She couldn't bear to let Ryan know she ever questioned her decision to marry him. Instead, she told him she was simply overwhelmed by the day's events and needed time to decompress. She never meant to worry him, let alone plan to be trapped in the snow with no means to contact him. The emphasis of her story focused on Emma and the strange encounter Savy experienced.

"Sounds like you were right about the exhaust poisoning your brain." He held her close. "You could have died sitting in a car like that, Sav."

"But that's the thing, I didn't sit in my car." She turned to look into his eyes. "It wasn't a dream or some wild hallucination, Ryan. I know that as well as I know my own name."

He stroked her hair. "I believe you believe Emma was real, but think about it, Sav. It's impossible."

"What about the angel?" She mindlessly ran her fingers along his arm, pondering every detail of her encounter. "How could I have known what you said about her?"

"Intuitive guess maybe? I don't know, sweetheart, but if Emma took care of you, I'm forever in her debt." He squeezed Savy's leg. "What do you say we go out for a nice dinner to celebrate our engagement?"

"I am getting a little hungry." She admired her ring. "And I'd love go out on the arm of my handsome fiancé." She paused. "But I have nothing here to wear except my ruined red silk dress or my yoga pants."

"Oh? I think I can help you with that dilemma." He stood, then walked over to the closet and pulled out two more boxes. "Merry Christmas, babe."

"Oh Ryan, you've given me so much already."

"I was saving these for your birthday next month, but what's wrong with a man spoiling his wife-to-be?" His eyes narrowed. "Now go try them on. If they fit and you like them, do we have a date?"

Savy nodded and offered a coy smile then kissed his cheek before prancing back to the bedroom.

§

She returned a few minutes later donning a cobalt cocktail dress that accentuated her sparkling blue eyes and a pair of black Prada platform pumps.

"Are you ready for a night on the town?" Ryan reached into the closet for Savy's cashmere coat, helped her into it.

Feeling something hard in the pocket, she pulled it out. "It's Emma's present." She inspected the gift rolling it over in her hands.

Ryan looked at her in consternation. "You never mentioned a--"

"Don't you see, Ryan? This proves that Emma was real." She held the small box up to him. "Emma gave me this after breakfast this morning, just before I left. I stuffed it in my pocket and with everything else, I completely forgot about it."

Ryan rubbed the stubbles on his chin. "Okay, now you have me curious." He chuckled. "Lets see what's inside."

Ripping off the paper, Savy opened the box and peered inside. A beautiful platinum locket lay on the mound of snow-white cotton. The heart was etched with intricate lettering. "It's stunning." She ran her fingers across the letters then dangled the charm from its chain to admire it. "S--E--B. I guess Emma must have been her middle name."

"Sav." Ryan stared at the heart-shaped keepsake. "Those are your initials." He inspected the locket more carefully then opened it to reveal two pictures. "Look at this, Savannah."

She glared in disbelief at the two small photos inside of her necklace...the right side held a picture of her and the left a photograph of Ryan. "Have you ever seen these pictures before?"

"No, I haven't." He scratched his head. "And I don't remember posing for them either."

"Neither do I." She started to place the locket back in its box, then halted. What she thought was the bottom of the container was, instead, a handwritten note. Trembling, she glanced at the letter then handed the paper to her fiancé.

"I'm too freaked. You read it, Ryan."

Unfolding the missive, he began to read:

Dearest Savy,

I know what happened to me--to us--seems impossible, hence the definition of a miracle. So I wanted to explain how the gift you gave to me was far greater than you could imagine. You had to choose your own destiny, Savy. But when you accepted Ryan's proposal, you changed my destiny too, and my heart overflowed as a flood of new memories swirled into my mind. Thank you for giving me the life and the family I lost. Be happy, Savy, and love with all of your heart as I know you will.
Savannah Emily (Emma) Bradford Patterson

Savy shivered, holding her hands together with the locket between them. "You mean...I am Emma?"

"I think it's more like Emma is you." Ryan folded the paper, placed it back in the box then he took the locket from Savy and fastened it around her neck. "Whatever happened to you last night was miraculous, Sav. Somehow you altered your future." He chuckled. "But we'd best keep that to ourselves." He kissed her cheek then held his hand out. "You ready to go?"

Savy tucked a strand of hair behind her ear. "Emma is the one who gave me the gift." She took Ryan's hand then nuzzled into him as they walked out the door together. "Merry Christmas, Emma," she whispered softly.

After Midnight

Book Three

Casi McLean

After Midnight

"In case you haven't noticed, I don't play by the rules." Derek ran the edge of the cold switchblade across Sabrina's neck with just enough pressure to force the lump clenching her throat into her stomach. "Not that I didn't enjoy playing the part of your devoted boyfriend." He raked his fingers through her thick, auburn hair, tightened his fist then pulled her head into his chest.

Her heart raced, beat so hard against the knife she felt sure he could see it pulsate. "So you're going to––"

"Kill you?" He finished her question before she had a chance to sputter the words. "Damn your officious interference ...what the hell possessed you to leave a party you're emceeing to come back here on New Year's Eve?"

§

That was the million-dollar question. Maybe she had been possessed. No reasonable analysis of the last eleven months made sense. It defied logic. And Sabrina had always relied on her sense of logic. Even as a child, understanding the why and how of things had driven her, fed an insatiable hunger through school and lured her into a career where billions of dollars spun through cyberspace daily. Equities, options, commodities––the intrigue of the market fascinated her.

At twenty-eight, she knew more about trading than most seasoned professionals and landed a key position at ICE, the Atlanta-based Intercontinental Exchange. But the dream job came at a price. While Sabrina's genius opened doors to a promising future, it cocooned her, isolated her into an emotional prison. She ate, breathed, and dreamed work--until last Valentines Day.

The dreary Saturday deepened her loneliness. Not that she had any desire for sentimental cards, candy or flowers, but in the silence of an empty house, she fanaticized awakening in the arms of a hot, sensual man. A man who would take her, intoxicate her with passion. The mere thought stirred her desire. She shifted in her chair as a warm tingle crept over her. After all, despite her intellect, she was still a woman.

By college, she'd had the male species figured out. Testosterone drove their behavior, and while she enjoyed the pleasure they could evoke, she'd resigned that once their trophy was conquered, they set their sights on a new mark. The pattern had duplicated exactly the same with every encounter she'd experienced. She knew what to expect and felt comfortable selecting occasional subjects to fulfill her sporadic hedonistic needs. Aside from that, Brie didn't do relationships. Emotions defied logic too, and yet, there were times she dreamed of finding a man who would love her for who she was, not what she provided for him.

Most holidays distracted her. Socializing kept her from dwelling on the hole in her otherwise successful, logical life. Thanksgiving, Christmas and forth of July, her brother Conner's family took the foreground. Sabrina spoiled her niece, Kayla, who gave her a sense of family. New Years Eve was generally spent flitting place-to-place putting in face time at various business events, which served to mask the void lurking deep within her heart, the glaring reality that her workaholic lifestyle sabotaged any hope of her ever finding love.

But Valentines Day brought the emptiness front and center, especially when it fell on a weekend. She tried to distract herself, lit a fire, snuggled into her favorite chair and, wrapping her hands around a warm cup of coffee, sipped the steamy brew while she watched the flames dance up the flu. But the cold, drizzly day still slunk around her like a shroud reminding her of how utterly alone she was.

When the doorbell rang, she set the cup aside, rushed to the door hopeful that whoever stood behind it would provide some diversion from her depressing mood.

"Package for Miss"--the delivery man glanced down at his parcel--"Sabrina Wentworth?"

Brie reached for the box. "That would be me."

"Sign here first, Ma'am." He handed her a signature device.

She scrawled her name with her forefinger, thanked him as she received the parcel, then closed the door, her mind spinning on acknowledgement of the return addressee's name. Bemused, she curled up in her chair again, stared at the box in disbelief for several moments before slipping her finger under the edge of the brown paper wrapping.

How could Aunt Kathy have sent Brie a package? Her aunt had disappeared without a trace ten years earlier and, after a lengthy and intense investigation, the unsolved case closed. By all indications, Kathleen Wentworth was randomly targeted that New Year's Eve, perhaps by some drunken admirer ringing in the new year. The detectives concurred she was kidnapped, and presumed murdered.

Sabrina peeled back the paper, opened the oversized shoebox, reached beneath soft pink tissue paper and pulled out a beautiful anniversary clock. She'd seen the timepiece before, watched it for hours when it was new, mesmerized by the visible inner workings and how impossible it seemed the spring only needed winding once a year to keep the pendulum spinning to-and-fro with precision.

Aunt Kathy warned her never to touch the fragile workings or the clock would stop. It was Sabrina's childhood curiosity that had broken the spindle. Yet her aunt never punished her. Instead, she still cherished the timepiece, kept it on the mantel silent and still for as long as Brie could remember.

Had the gift been among Aunt Kathy's belongings after her disappearance, Brie wondered? She couldn't remember. She centered the base on the mantle, gently attached the golden pendulum that was neatly encased in its own tissue paper to the delicate spindle. Then she turned the key, setting the weights in motion as she'd seen her aunt do. She mimicked the process with rote precision then stared at the glistening gold bob as it spun back-and-forth.

Why now, she wondered, ten years after her aunt's disappearance? How was it even possible? Could Kathy still be alive? Brie's mind swirled with mounting questions. A surge of emotion washed over her, pooled in her eyes until a single tear escaped, streamed down her cheek, puddled onto the tissue paper.

Wrapped up in her busy life, she rarely had time to think of anything beyond her own issues. A wave of guilt flashed over Brie as she muddled through memories. Kathleen Wentworth never had children, but she'd cherished Sabrina, loved her and Conner as if she had given birth to them.

Brie's face went pale. "Conner," she whispered. Had he received an unexpected gift from his aunt as well? She dug into her pocket for her cell phone. "Call Conner Wentworth."

"Happy Valentines Day, Sis." His cheerful voice somehow soothed her fragile nerves.

After a lengthy explanation of her mysterious package and confirmation that Conner had no such delivery, the two bantered back-and-forth about their aunt.

"Let it go, Brie. You'll drive yourself crazy trying to find answers where there are none."

She'd expected her brother's analysis, accept what you know and let go of the rest. But Sabrina was never able to dismiss unanswered questions. She would find the answers; unravel her aunt's disappearance if it took a lifetime. After they said their goodbyes, she stuffed her cell phone back in her robe pocket, placed the dome over her cherished gift and watched as the pendulum spun, then slowed to a stop. It figured. The spindle was never repaired. She'd have the clock refurbished when she got around to it but for now, just having the clock on the mantel made her feel closer to her aunt.

The delivery certainly distracted Brie. Forgetting the holiday and her loveless life, she spent the entire day and night sifting through what was left of her aunt's possessions, determined to find some clue to her mysterious disappearance. She ripped open stacks of boxes she'd carefully packed and carted from Aunt Kathy's home. The contents of the dusty cartons left piled in her spare bedroom for over nine years now lay helter-skelter across the floor in Sabrina's organized chaos. A stream of white boards attached to the walls came alive with schematics resembling an askew timeline, color-coded with Brie's unique categories.

By ten p.m. she felt physically and emotionally exhausted. Before flipping off the light, she glanced at her handiwork, murmured to herself, "Rome wasn't built in a day" then closed the spare room door. Her mind still ruminating, she turned on the shower, dimmed the bathroom lights, slipped beneath the cascading waterfall. Steamy water streamed over her shoulders, soothed her. She closed her eyes, squeezed the soapy mesh sponge sending soft suds slithering over her wet skin. Thoughts of her aunt drifted into the corners of her mind as her sensuality awakened. When she slid between her freshly cleaned moss-green sheets Brie felt so relaxed, so lascivious, she immediately drifted into sensuous slumber.

§

Yes, Valentines Day, that's when the dreams began. The moment her head hit the pillow, she mystically entered another world--his world. His arms and legs entangled around her, warm skin pressing against hers, hands roving over her naked body. The heat between them burned, seethed like nothing she'd ever felt before. Her body writhed with pleasure, succumbed in complete surrender. Logic told her the dream would end, but heightened sensuality, her rapid pulse and euphoric reactions felt all too real and she fought to linger in her illicit dream.

Brie had no idea who her fantasy lover was, but she didn't care. She craved his embrace, his touch. His soft lips ran up her neck then opened over hers. His muscular chest slid over her breasts. He lifted her, rolled her onto him. Clinging with unbridled desire, she ran her fingers through his thick mane and melted into him. Should she dare to open her eyes? Or would that rip him away, cast her illusory paramour into a mist of forgotten dreams?

She had to open her eyes if nothing more than a tiny slit. She needed to see him, to memorize his features, tuck them into her memory so that when she awoke she'd remember every moment of this incredible dream. She pried her eyes open, peeked through her eyelashes at first. Even in the dim light his bronzed skin glistened. She tilted her head back and, with eyes wide open now, gazed into ebony eyes framed by his tousled raven hair.

"Can't you feel the connection between us? We are"-- he paused for a moment--"kismet, Bria. Our souls are entwined." He slid her off his chest, lay on his side then, perching his elbow on lavender satin sheets, rested his chin on the palm of his hand and searched deep into her azure eyes.

"Fate?" she finally dared to whisper. "Destiny is merely what you make of it."

"Yes. But when a door has opened, there is rarely a second chance to walk through it." His crooked his finger grazed her cheek.

"But--"

When she began to speak, he placed his fingertip over her lips. "I know you can't wrap your head around the idea--yet. But can you trust me?"

"I . . ." She paused, unsure of why she knew the answer to that question without forethought. "Of course I do," she said in earnest. Brie didn't even know this man's name, but somehow she knew she could trust him with her life. How odd. In the dog-eat-dog world she lived in, outside of her dreams, she trusted very few people. She kissed the finger still resting on her lips then pulled herself up and hugged him, her long auburn hair draping his shoulders.

"Then we will just take one day at a time. And speaking about time, we should probably get showered. Do you want to go first, or shall I?" He kissed her cheek. "We've got a lot to do today, remember?"

Brie remembered nothing about any of this, but that's how dreams worked, right? No rationale, no normalcy, one could fly, slay dragons or kill ghosts in the cosmic nirvana of dreams. She wondered what it would be like to fly high above the city in this man's arms like Lois Lane had done with Superman.

"You go ahead." She snuggled into the warm bed, marveled at his musculature completely beguiled until he disappeared into the bathroom. Who was this amazing man? No matter. He'd been conjured from the canyons of her mind, probably the coalescence of qualities she desired in a man ...if she were to want a man at all, which seemed a waste of time to her. The drama and concessions one had to endure in relationships that statistically would fail anyway made coveting a union analytically detrimental.

She glanced around the room, paused at the sight of a wallet that lay on the bedside table. His driver's license should provide some information, at least his name, she thought, reaching for the billfold. The moment she grasped it, the wallet began to vibrate then burst into mellow harp music. She immediately dropped it, stared at her cell phone lying next to her atop her moss-green sheets, the alarm wailing.

"Damn." She tucked her sweat-dampened hair behind her ears aware she'd been asleep, but visceral responses lingered, sensuous arousal that felt as real as any she'd ever known. And she wanted more.

§

Brie got her wish. Aidan, the name she instinctively knew upon her next visit, came to her in dreams every night thereafter. She lived every day in her real life as usual, monitoring the market by day, falling asleep in her own bed atop moss-green sheets, then awakened on lavender satin, wrapped in his arms. Conversely, when she fell asleep with Aidan, she'd wake up in the real world, return to the exciting, high-tech cyber-market, monitoring billions in trades and protecting insider secrets.

In her fantasy world, Brie's career advanced down a different path. Still driven by the need to find answers, she'd become an expert investigative reporter. And despite owning the knowledge her dreamscape most likely had evolved through some intrinsic subconscious need, she looked forward to waking on lavender sheets and the quiet purr Aidan made as he slept. She'd never imagined how content, how comfortable she could feel just having him there to support or encourage her, and how passionate intimacy could be with the right person.

But she was acutely aware that Aidan didn't really exist. And though she'd imagined the perfect man for her, reality held no such perfection. As long as she had her fantasy, she didn't need real, did she? Maybe her imagination held her sanity in balance through her subconscious, comforting her with a satisfying fantasy to counteract the absence of love in her life?

Sleep, she remotely remembered the feeling, but had she slept at all since Valentine's Day? It had been three months since the cycle began. No matter which bed she crawled into at night, moss green or lavender, the moment she drifted off, she'd awaken in the other. Sleepless perhaps, yet she'd never felt tired. Still, if her subconscious was trying to send her a message, shouldn't she listen?

It was May 5 when Derek Mills swooped into her life. The recently hired ICE IT analyst was handsome, dashing and a little overwhelming at times, especially when it came to pursuing her. She knew it was completely bizarre her interest in Derek had her feeling guilty, as if she were cheating on Aidan. He didn't even exist, not in the real world anyway. But that's how she felt. Like she was plotting an illicit affair behind his back.

Sabrina's mouth dropped as she threw her office door open.

"Have I gotten your attention yet?" Derek arched an eyebrow, offering a wry smile.

"Are you kidding me?" She strode through the entry, closed the door behind her. "This is an embarrassing display of roses." She shook her head, walked around the desk toward her chair where he sat with a boyish ear-to-ear grin. Derek certainly had no qualms about being attracted to her. He plied her with little gifts, flirted relentlessly and nudged his way into her life little-by-little coaxing her to succumb to his charms. She resisted, of course, but her strong will softened with each encounter as if he chipped away another slice of her protective shell, or thawed it with unpredictable fervor. Nonetheless, it was Aidan who melted her heart.

§

Derek didn't give up easily. He pursued Sabrina with steadfast tenacity, showering her with little gifts and unrequited admiration. The fact that she didn't return his affections gnawed at him, but that only served to strengthen his resolve. Her position at ICE was the core to his plan. When he discovered that S.B. Wentworth was a woman, he felt elated at his stroke of luck.

Derek had always been able to charm the ladies. His innate good looks, sandy blonde hair and fiery brown eyes would catch any woman's eye, but added to his finely tuned muscular body and cocky attitude he had no problem having his way with them.

He used his assets to his advantage. His quick aptitude taught him there were two paths to success in life, the hard way and easy way, and the path of least resistance was much more lucrative. Using his charm to his best advantage was a no-brainer.

He had to admit that Princess Sabrina was a challenge, perhaps even a force to be reckoned with. When it came to the market, she didn't miss a beat, calculated and considered everything she did. He accepted her intelligence was far beyond his, but she was emotionally inept and that is where he excelled. Sabrina Wentworth was the key to the door of his future and he intended to unlock it.

Grabbing her hand, he pulled her onto his lap. "Haven't I proven myself by now? It's just a date Sabrina. I promise I won't bite."

"There's nothing to prove." She pulled herself upright and stood, glaring down at him. "Okay. I give up. I'll go out with you." She paused for a beat then added, "on one condition." Her scowl relaxed. "Promise me you'll conduct yourself appropriately during business hours. Interoffice fraternizing incites gossip and it's unprofessional. I've worked too hard to get where I am and I don't want to jeopardize my position."

Checkmate, he thought. A room filled with roses had delivered a queen to trap Sabrina's king. She didn't stand a chance. His smile deepened.

"Okay then, this Saturday night. I'll pick you up at seven and take you to one of my favorite restaurants. Have you ever been to the Capital Grille?"

"Yes, of course. You have excellent taste, Derek."

He had done his homework, memorized her likes and dislikes and was well aware of what he needed to do to turn Sabrina's head. She frequented the Capital Grille so the restaurant would become his preference as well.

Derek stood. Tempted to swoop her into his arms and plant a passionate kiss on her luscious lips, he thought better of the idea. This pursuit needed to be slow, methodical. She wasn't the type of woman that would jump into anything, especially a relationship.

"Madam." He cocked his head, tipped his imaginary hat. "I'll leave you to your work then." Walking toward the door, he paused, turned back and said, "Don't forget to take time to smell the roses." Smiling at his own wit, he disappeared, closing the door behind him.

But dating Sabrina wasn't as easy as he thought it would be. He misjudged her. She wasn't simply emotionally inept; she was downright frigid. Derek wasn't used to being shut down. In the past, he could have his choice of any woman he desired and it took little time to have her between the sheets. For some reason Sabrina seemed immune to his charms. His typical plan of wining and dining fell short at the punch line. Even his best lines had little effect on her. No matter. He could scratch his itch in other places.

Sabrina was a means to an end. Gaining her trust far outweighed a hook up. So Derek would be whatever she needed him to be. Once he had her in the palm of his hand, he had access to her computer, her passwords and, most importantly, her safe, which held insider trade secrets. With that knowledge he could trade the market with an edge, make millions with a simple, strategically placed click. And the best part, his trades could be scattered through options, hidden in cyberspace, unnoticed.

The ease of personal trading brought the opportunities to his fingertips. Trades went through effortlessly for an individual who understood the premise, and the software-- his expertise. His chosen profession as an IT analyst opened doors to a prosperous future--even if he entered them illegally. There was no way Derek would accept a menial position figuring out answers to other people's problems. He refused to fulfill his father's drunken predictions. His sharp words haunted Derek, driven him. "You'll never amount to more than someone else's pencil pusher." All Derek needed was a foot in the door. A few algorithms and click, he would be an instant millionaire.

No one would ever suspect him of insider trading. If anything, they would assume he just hit a lucky streak. He would distract Sabrina just long enough to start his bankroll. Then he would dump her, move on to his next mark. He wouldn't be greedy. Greed could arouse unnecessary suspicion. He would get in and out, then quit his job, maybe even leave the state. A sadistic smirk emerged as he thought about his flawless plan. The timing had to be perfect. So he would wait, watch, take everything in when the opportunities arose and, when the stars aligned, he would strike like a coiled cobra, then slither away.

§

Sabrina tried to analyze her situation, but no analysis could provide answers to her bizarre situation. She and Derek seemed to be a good fit. He understood her world and, if she were truthful with herself, she would admit that colleagues took her a little more seriously when she entered an event on the arm of a man. Her chosen career landed her smack dab in the middle of a male dominated industry, and she learned all too quickly that chauvinism and sexual harassment still thrived in the world of big business. Derek provided her an umbrella in the storm of testosterone.

She spent free evenings sifting through her aunt's possessions. Her inexplicable disappearance became an obsession for Sabrina. The police and their cold case files proved useless. They were unable or at least unwilling to provide Sabrina with any information beyond that already filed in public records. But the more time she spent in Aidan's world, the more determined she was to find answers about her aunt.

Piles of papers covered Sabrina's floor, but so far nothing had revealed even a hint about what could have happened to Kathleen Wentworth. Perhaps the police were right to give up the search, Sabrina thought, as she flipped through the pages of some old books. The last carton was nearly empty. She shivered thinking how easily she could've missed the small leather-bound diary at the bottom of the box.

She opened the journal, ran her fingers down the yellowed pages across her aunt's handwriting and began to read. A moment later she fell completely spellbound.

Edward came to me again last night, his touch stirred desire I never knew I possessed. If only my dreams were as real in daylight as they are when I am in his arms. The burning passion between us warms my heart during my waking hours, but I long to retire at night, praying my dreams continue.

Sabrina held the diary close to her chest. Had her aunt experienced passionate dreams as well? She leaned against the wall, slowly slid down to the floor and continued reading. The similarities were uncanny. Questions began to find answers.

I finally told Edward of my dreams. I feared he'd think me mad, but his fascination with time and space eclipsed any skepticism he might have felt. He's determined to reveal the source of the portal between our worlds and vows he'll find a way we can be together.

Aunt Kathy's passion radiated from every page. The words enchanted Sabrina, enticed her into her aunt's love story so deeply she could almost hear her whispers. She closed the tattered diary, ran her fingers across the worn leather binding. Her mind swirled as she mused over the secret confessions, trying desperately to piece together fragmented memories and synthesize them into her own life. Like following a tiny trail of breadcrumbs, she had to find her way--figure out the riddle. The mystical connection between her aunt and herself grew more and more undeniable as she read the diary. The story defied logic, contradicted everything Sabrina knew to be real, but so did her own dreams.

And so her dual life continued, Derek in one world and Aidan in the other. A high-tech cyber prodigy by day and a super-sleuth investigative reporter by night ...or was it the other way around? At first there was no question which world existed in reality, but as time marched forward the line that separated her two lives grew more and more obscure.

Her passion for the expeditious Global market faded, yielded to a different kind of passion, the harmonious burning desire she found in Aidan's embrace. Moments with Derek paled in comparison. Though she enjoyed his company and cognitively knew he was the only living, breathing version of a man in her life, she couldn't bear to give herself to him.

Her time with Aidan dominated her thoughts--her heart--while the job she'd loved, worked for all her life, lost its luster like the dull finish of a tarnished antique. Sabrina couldn't wait to awaken on lavender satin. And the curious intrigue of an investigative reporter became more and more captivating.

Determined to keep her teleportation, for lack of a better word, a secret, she continued her research in both worlds, silently, never uttering a word about the bizarre dual life she led. She identified with her aunt. If Derek ever discovered what she believed to be true, he would surely her think her stark raving mad. And as close as she felt to Aidan, he probably would too. She couldn't tell either of them.

Aidan let out a low whistle, tossed the morning paper aside, then leaned over and began nibbling on Sabrina's neck.

"I'm going for a run. Care to join me?" He smoothed the hair away from her sleep-drenched eyes. "Unless of course you can think of a better exercise this morning."

She purred, pulling him closer, welcomed his mouth as it lingered over hers. He clasped both of her hands interlacing their fingers and stretched her arms high above her head, hovered over her, then descended. Her passion ignited. How could any part of this be unreal, Sabrina wondered. She wanted to be with Aidan, stay with him and mingle their lives.

When they had showered and sat down to breakfast, Sabrina mused over their intimate morning. Aidan, however, had his nose buried in the newspaper again.

"So what sparked your attention in the paper this morning?"

"Just reading about the latest Wall Street scandal." He shook his head. "It takes a lot of brass to pull off a Ponzi scheme like this." He placed the paper on the table beside her, pointed to the article. "Have you ever done a piece on the market or stockbrokers?"

"No," she paused a beat to make sure she kept her lavender-sheet identity intact. "But it might be interesting." She glanced down at the paper, scanned the highlights.

"Uncovering a scheme like that would be right up your alley. It could get global attention." He leaned back in his chair. "But I suppose it would be easier to investigate market greed if you lived in Chicago or New York."

"Right." She thought about ICE, but considered it better not to mention the local exchange. "It's something to consider, but I have my hands full right now with open investigations."

That was the truth. Sabrina had plenty to investigate regarding her aunt's disappearance, not to mention her mystical teleportation. But the diary at least proved she wasn't crazy––though from what she read so far, her aunt may have been. Perhaps the dreams were genetic phenomena. But if that were true, wouldn't she have experienced dream transfers her whole life? How had her perfectly logical life suddenly become so mystifying? Glancing back the paper, she scanned down the column. Her adrenalin exploded as her eyes froze on the name Derek Mills.

§

Sabrina awoke upon her drab-green sheets. It was almost Christmas and there was so much she had to do before the holidays. Tom Morgan, her direct boss, assigned to her the daunting task of setting up ICE's annual New Year's Eve party, which was a formidable undertaking in itself for someone who had to force herself to be a social butterfly. She had already secured the Wyndham Atlanta Galleria's Berkshire Ballroom, which accommodated approximately 450 guests. It would do quite nicely.

The facility often held elegant events and was within shouting distance of ICE. But Morgan gave her an endless laundry list of to-dos, which took her focus off the market where it belonged. And with Christmas gifts yet to be purchased for Kayla, Connor and Marissa, her brother's wife, Sabrina felt a bit overwhelmed.

Derek monopolized much more of her time of late and insisted on having a cozy dinner at her place on Christmas Eve. It was easy enough to have the meal catered, but she'd have to come up with a suitable menu and decor, elegant but not seductive. Why Derek chose her home instead of his was beyond her, but she assumed the request appropriate for a typical relationship. Had it been Aidan's request she would have jumped at the chance to prepare an intimate romantic dinner for two. But for Derek she simply smiled and agreed.

"To us." Derek held his wine glass up and clinked it to hers, sipped, then leaned against the mantel. "And may the coming year be prosperous for both of us."

"To us," she mimicked, while her thoughts flew to visions of Aidan.

"That's an interesting clock, Sabrina." He ran his fingers over the golden base. "Is it an antique?"

Her gaze focused on the clock beyond him. "I suppose. It was a gift from my aunt." Sabrina stared at the anniversary clock, the pendulum as it slowly turn. "That's odd."

"What?" Derek's brow narrowed into an inquisitive glare.

"It's been broken for years, but now it appears to be working." She moved forward to inspect the clock more closely.

"I must be good luck." Derek chuckled. He took her advance toward him as a come-on, grabbed her hand and led her to the sofa. "You've planned quite an event for New Year's Eve. I know you will be busy, but you will still be my date, won't you?"

"Of course." She felt a momentary flash of guilt. This Derek treated her well and seemed genuinely intrigued with her. Aidan lived in her dream world. The treacherous Derek she read about in the newspaper didn't exist here. Obviously her subconscious transferred unintentional negative feelings about him, created a monster of sorts, to justify her guilt for loving Aidan. Derek never gave her any reason to doubt him. He was thoughtful, sensitive, and treated her like a princess. Still, if she had a choice there was no doubt in her mind she would choose Aidan. Why couldn't Aidan be her reality?

§

Derek slipped his switchblade into the inside pocket of his tux jacket, peered into the mirror and straightened his tie, smirking at his ingenuity. Suggesting to Morgan that Sabrina be in charge of the black-tie event was genius if he did say so himself. And her inept romantic experience made her an easy pawn to manipulate.

She had no idea he handpicked the event location and placed the seed in her mind. An elegant lunch followed by a stroll around the grounds took care of that. The Wyndham Atlanta, so close to ICE he could spit on it. And the piece de resistance: he'd have a perfect alibi.

As Sabrina's date, he'd be beyond suspicion. She would be so monopolized by her schedule, he'd have plenty of opportunity to borrow her keycard, break into ICE, slip into her office, photograph the information he required and return to the party unnoticed. No one needed to get hurt. He patted the breast of his jacket reaffirming that his stealth switchblade was still there. Just in case, he thought.

So far, his plan evolved more smoothly than he'd imagined, especially his clever strategy to gain access to files that held highly classified corporate secrets. What woman didn't have a soft spot for romance? Sabrina's assistant was swept away when he appeared at the door with twelve dozen roses in tow. She didn't think twice about opening the door to Sabrina's office for him.

Once inside, Derek found the trigger to a false wall that revealed her safe. He had what he needed and, at the same time, set up an infallible rapport, all under the guise of a smitten romantic gesture, a display of roses for his darling Sabrina. And she was so taken aback at his exploit, it never occurred to her to mistrust his intentions.

The strategic setup took a mere moment to execute. The only snafu was the months of wining and dining Sabrina, prying clues out of her that would help him unlock her safe. That was a challenge, but well worth his efforts. Everything fell into place perfectly, and what better subterfuge than The New Year's Eve gala? The timing couldn't have been better if he'd planned the holiday himself.

As he drove to Sabrina's house, his thoughts ruminated over every scenario he could imagine for the evening. He covered all the bases leaving nothing to chance. Adrenaline pumped through his veins like high-octane fuel. His nervous system flew into overdrive, but it didn't dull his senses. To the contrary, he felt hyper alert, aware of his surroundings with acute detail.

His heart pounded. It was a high he'd never experienced before, despite his adolescent experimentation with drugs. By the time he and Sabrina reached the Wyndham, he knew he had to take the edge off, so when Sabrina excused herself to check on the caterers and make sure every detail was executed per her explicit directions, Derek shot straight to the open bar.

"Jamison. Neat." He tapped his fingers on the cold granite surface. "Two fingers," he added, slightly loosening his tie.

"Sure thing, Sir." The bartender set a napkin and glass in front of Derek then, with memorized expertise, poured two ounces of premium whiskey. "Big event here tonight."

"You have no idea." He swigged the Jamison down in two gulps, placed the glass on the bar. After drawing in a deep breath he chuckled. "New Year's Eve should always be a big deal, right?" He retightened his tie. "Happy New Year." He tipped his imaginary hat and headed toward the ballroom.

"Happy New Year." The bartender's reply echoed in the distance.

Derek wasn't sure when it would come, but knew he'd recognize his opportunity when it arose. All through dinner he played the roll of the attentive boyfriend. When Sabrina excused herself to set up the announcements he almost split, but thought better of the idea. The best time to leave would be shortly before midnight.

Sabrina wasn't the type to go searching for a kiss at the stroke of twelve. She'd be more interested in the punctual release of balloons and making sure everyone had a glass of champagne. The company guests would be grabbing their partner and watching the midnight countdown on a giant TV screen, the 800lb Atlanta peach drifting down to mark the beginning of the new year. So he waited patiently.

§

Sabrina smiled as she watched Derek from across the room. She was nothing if not competent. Every detail of the gala had it's own manager, the balloons at midnight, the champagne, she orchestrated everything precisely and the evening ran as beautifully as a finally tuned timepiece.

Everything occurred according to plan--that is everything except Derek. Ever since she read that newspaper article, she couldn't shake the feeling that something about Derek made her skin crawl.

At first she shrugged it off, attributed the whole idea into her wild imagination. But the more she watched him when he was unaware of her observation, the more she realized her intuition had credibility. He was slick. His smooth talking charmed whomever he directed his attention, but the abrupt scowl on his face when his target turned away was nothing short of devious. He had an agenda. Sabrina wasn't sure what he had up his sleeve, but she was determined to find out, tonight.

She sensed his agitation when he'd picked her up this evening, and as they walked into the Wyndham, he grabbed her arm with a clammy hand. Forty degrees outside and his brow glistened with beads of sweat. The moment she excused herself he shot straight into the bar and downed a double shot of whiskey with a single swig. The man was definitely up to something and whatever he planned was eminent.

Sabrina pulled her cell phone out of her handbag. Almost 11:30. Placing the phone back in her purse, she noticed that her keycard was missing. She leaned over, whispered into Derek's ear, "I have to go get ready for midnight." She kissed his cheek. "See you next year."

She giggled like a love-struck schoolgirl, playing innocent before she rushed off, vanished around the corner. The moment she was out of sight she wiped her mouth with the back of her hand as if slime had congealed across her lips. She hid in the dark shadows of an unlit hallway, peered around at her date.

Derek instantly excused himself, scooted out of the ballroom and hurried down a hallway toward the exit. Sabrina flew right behind him, lurking in the shadows. She mimicked his every move.

When he headed straight for ICE, she realized how accurate her instincts were. She watched him pull her keycard from his pocket, swipe it, then dash toward the elevator. Barley clearing the door before it slammed after her, she scooted behind the abandoned security desk.

With all the company's executives only a few steps away, the CEO had no problem giving the security staff the evening off. She rolled her eyes in disapproval. Derek stepped into the elevator. The moment the doors closed, Sabrina pressed the silent alarm under the desk then tore toward the stairwell. She knew exactly where her bogus paramour was headed.

She darted up the steps, exited at the fifth floor, creeping toward her office. The door still ajar, she peeked inside to see Derek pressing against her safe. He handled himself with the skill and expertise of a seasoned thief; even down to the thumbprint he apparently lifted from her right thumb and somehow created a duplicate.

Flipping through her files he scanned page after page, pulled out one or two at a time, placed them on the desk just long enough to snap a picture before returning them to the folders.

"No one ever would've known," she whispered, leaned back against the wall.

Derek must've heard the shuffle from her dress, or a slight creak of the door as she moved away. A moment later his right hand covered her mouth, while his left held a switchblade to her neck. When she squirmed to get free he only tightened his grip, pressed the icy blade deeper into her throat.

"You promise not to scream and I'll consider removing my hand from your mouth."

She shook her head in agreement and he slowly released his hold.

"You won't hurt me Derek. You're not a killer." She tried to swallow, but he yanked her hair, tilted her head back. "You said that you loved me." Her raspy voice croaked.

"In case you haven't noticed, I don't play by the rules." Derek ran the edge of the cold switchblade across Sabrina's neck with just enough pressure to force the lump clenching her throat into her stomach. "Not that I didn't enjoy playing the part of your devoted boyfriend." He raked his fingers through her thick, auburn hair, tightened his fist then pulled her head into his chest.

Her heart raced, beat so hard against the knife she felt sure he could see it pulsate. "So you're going to--"

"Kill you?" He finished her question before she had a chance to sputter the words. "Damn your officious interference ...what the hell possessed you to leave a party you're emceeing to come back here on New Year's Eve?"

"I guess you weren't as deceptive as you thought you were."

"No one was supposed to get hurt. Why couldn't you have just left well enough alone?" He pulled out her office chair, slammed her into the seat then lifted his foot and shoved the stool against the wall.

"It's over, Derek." She sputtered, coughed as she spoke. "The police are on the way, probably entering the building as we speak.

Before she finished the sentence the elevator door opening broke through the hallway silence, followed by a rush of footsteps in the corridor. Derek turned toward the door, his switchblade hovering over Sabrina's throat.

Sabrina shuttered, glanced at the clock on the wall. Midnight. "Oh Aidan. I can't lose you. With all my heart I want to be with you." She clenched her eyes tightly and drew in a last breath as the switchblade thrust deeper into her neck.

"Take one step closer and she's dead," Derek spit out.

"Who?" The detective held his gun with both hands aiming directly at Derek's chest.

"If I die she'll go with me." His eyes shifted to Sabrina, but all he saw was an empty chair. "What the hell?"

§

Sabrina clung to Aidan's neck, pressed her head tightly against his chest until she could hear the beating of his heart.

"You're here." Tears welled beneath her eyes, trickled down her cheeks. "I almost lost you."

"It was just a dream, Bria. You will never lose me." He gently stroked her hair and held her close. "You're okay now."

She was okay now, but she hadn't been dreaming. When she read the last entries in her aunt's diary, she finally understood what happened to Kathleen Wentworth--and why her dreams of Aidan felt so real. According to Edward, the anniversary clock somehow created a link--a portal between alternate worlds.

The presence of the clock activated her aunt's dreams just as it triggered Sabrina's. But the key to the portal was the glistening gold bob. When the mystical pendulum began to spin back-and-forth on Christmas Eve, it initiated a countdown of sorts; the point at which the barrier between worlds would become so thin, a person could pass through it.

Her aunt's scribbling made no logical sense, defied everything Sabrina knew to be valid. But with everything that happened she had to conclude that perhaps forces existed in the universe that contradicted logic. If Edward's analysis was accurate, Kathleen Wentworth didn't die. She transported to another reality, a world where she could be with Edward--Aidan's world. Which meant Sabrina had one chance to be with Aidan, the stroke of midnight on New Year's Eve.

She trembled at the thought of how close she came to losing the love of her life. If the police hadn't showed up at her office at precisely 12:00, if she hadn't glanced up at the clock ...but what mystified her was that she hadn't gone to bed or awakened on Aidan's lavender sheets, yet somehow her desperate plea to be with him at the stoke of twelve teleported her--no shifted her to the other side of midnight.

Sabrina cuddled into Aidan's warm chest. The whole melding between worlds might take a bit of adjustment, but she had a clean slate here and this time she would live her life immersed in a newly acquired passion.

Aidan awakened in her more than budding desire. He shattered the fortress surrounding her heart, set free the compassion her father stifled in her childhood when he walked out on her pregnant mother and her brother Colin. Bria finally felt love.

She would never wake up on drab green sheets again, never enter the doors of ICE or play fast and free with the jet set. But she didn't care. She loved Aidan, knew he loved her. And investigative reporting fascinated her, especially after her brief encounter with Derek. The idea of exposing bad guys and helping people at the same time thrilled her.

And Aunt Kathy, Sabrina couldn't wait to see her, compare notes. The only hesitation Bria felt about transferring worlds centered on Kayla. Had her beautiful niece been born to this world too? And if so, could they build the same bond? Sabrina couldn't bear to leave that to chance, so just in case she left a note with her lawyer to deliver her aunt's diary and antique anniversary clock to Miss Kayla Wentworth on Valentine's Day of her 28th year.

Convergent

Book Four

Casi McLean

Convergent

"Control that bleeding ...suction ...this child will not bleed out on my watch." When the team had done everything they could, Sierra squeezed her eyes, bit her bottom lip retracing every detail in her mind, and waited. She'd preformed the procedure with rote precision. But the organ was in transit for almost six hours. Lack of blood flow for that length of time could take its toll and––she felt the twitch.

After holding her breath in silence through dragging seconds, she assessed the muscle as it began to beat, pump life back into three-year-old Brooklyn McArthur.

"Yes." The tension drained from Sierra's face and a high washed over her the likes of which no addictive fix could possibly evoke. "We've got a rhythm."

The rush never diminished. Regardless of who lay on her operating table, whenever she a held a heart in her hand, surgically reconnected tissue to a virtually lifeless patient dependent entirely on cardio-pulmonary by-pass, she felt a surge of adrenalin explode through her as if the procedure injected life force into her own body.

But this surgery felt different somehow. Brooklyn tugged on Sierra's heartstrings and she had a difficult time distancing herself despite her decisive professionalism. She couldn't bear the thought of the unspeakable. Not every case had a happy ending. Normally, Sierra wouldn't allow herself to think about failures, the lives she couldn't repair, revive or resurrect. She objectively compartmentalized those into educational experiences. A heart surgeon needed to check emotions at the door, and Sierra learned well.

But Brooklyn McArthur pierced her armor, touched her soul like no patient before. How else could Sierra explain the extraordinary pull she'd felt when the child's father reached out to her three years later, pleaded for her to drop everything at Emory and fly to Honolulu to treat Brook's infection, a 4,500 mile, ten-hour flight.

"She's all I have left, Dr. Norton. I can't lose her too."

"What do you mean lose her too?"

"My wife, Alyssa, was killed in a car accident a few months after Brooklyn's surgery." His voice relaxed into compliance. "That's why I took a job in Hawaii. Brook and I grieved for a year. It was time for both of us to let go, get away from Atlanta and start over."

"I'm so sorry. I remember Alyssa. You two dealt with so much pain together over Brooklyn's illness. I can't imagine how difficult the last three years have been for you."

"There were some rough moments. Honestly, I don't know how I would have gotten through Alyssa's death if I didn't have Brook. But we're in a good place now." He cleared his throat.

"If I were to even entertain the idea, I'd need to see her records, and consult with her medical team. What have they told you?"

"I've already released her files, had them forwarded to you. The doctors are cautiously optimistic about Brooklyn's infection, but she believes you are the only one who can cure her. If there is any significance in the notion that her stated of mind could make a difference in her recovery, I have to indulge her. Please come. I'll pay for your flight, hotel and all your expenditures." Trenton McArthur paused to refuel. "Hey, how often do you get an offer for an all expense-paid trip to Hawaii?"

"There is that." Sierra softened, pulled her long dark hair off her neck. "And with Memorial Day this weekend only emergency surgeries would require my input." She paused a few moments to consider her schedule, her gut instincts to drop everything niggling at her. "I'll get someone to cover my patients for a few days and call you in a couple of hours with my flight plan. In the mean time, you tell Brooklyn I've got her back."

Six hours later, Sierra peered out the window of seat 3-A, watching the Atlanta Airport fade into the landscape as the nonstop Boeing 767 lifted off and soared into billowing clouds. The nonstop trip sailed smoothly over the mainland. Sierra caught up on her email, studied Brooklyn's digital files then watched a movie and fell asleep. But a few hours beyond the California coast, somewhere over the pacific, the jet encountered major turbulence that jolted her from slumber. Captain Murphy, the pilot, climbed to a higher elevation, but the inexorable storm swallowed the jumbo jet, pitched it to-and-fro like a tiny piper cub. He switched on the seatbelt sign then in a calm voice broke the silent tension gripping the passengers.

"I'm sure you've noticed a little turbulence the last fifteen minutes or so. This storm is a doozy, but we should be on the other side shortly and should land in Honolulu on time. Please relax and stay buckled in your seat until the turbulence subsides."

Sierra pushed down a fear of flying she'd never known before. Gripping the armrests, she stared out her rain-splattered window into ominous clouds. The electrical system fluttered as the plane lurched and battled obscurity. A lightening bolt sliced the sky, spewed a ball of glistening blue-green energy at the tail of the battered 767 that spun down the aisle, singed the seats in its path before piercing through the otherwise impenetrable cockpit.

Without warning the giant jet plunged, whipsawed the passengers. Screams drowned the clatter of oxygen masks tumbling from overhead compartments. An unsecured beverage cart skidded from the galley randomly scattering alcohol, soda and cups through the air as it flew down the aisle. The aircraft lunged sideways, flinging passengers like ragdolls, still bound at the waist by their seatbelts. Sierra Norton's head cracked against the window--then spun into oblivion.

"Are you okay?" His voice soothed the terror of imminent death from Sierra's thoughts. "Here, let me help you back to your seat."

The plane shuttered beneath her. Engines roared, mimicking the explosive thunder outside. The man easily lifted her and she collapsed against his muscular chest. Head throbbing, Sierra pried an eye open a slit, until the blood oozing from her head trickled in to blur her vision. She caught a glimpse of his handsome face, his sandy blond hair, and a hazy emblem on the collar of his military uniform.

Dabbing her forehead, he raised his voice to be heard over the incessant roar.

"That's a nasty gash. How do you feel?" He set her down on a cold, hard surface, not the comfortable seat she'd been strapped into before the aircraft preformed Blue-Angel somersaults.

"I'll be fine. Thanks." Sierra's hand flew to her forehead. Blood oozed from her hematoma, or more accurately, the two-inch laceration slashed into her head at the base of the lump. "It might help if I put a little ice on my head though." She took the cloth from his warm hand, pressed it on her wound.

"I'd like to indulge your request for ice, but . . ." His voice trailed off as he sat beside her.

When Sierra vision cleared, she stared blankly, went pale, her head spinning.

"You gals sure have guts, I'll give you that." The Commanding Officer shook his head side-to-side. "And a looker too."

"What the hell just happened here?" She squeezed her eyes shut then opened them again. Her jaw dropped at what she saw. An entire platoon of soldiers, male and female, most of whom appeared to be medics of some kind, and all prepared for combat, lined both walls of the small aircraft.

"You'll get used to the turbulence after you've chalked up a few missions, Nurse"--the CO glanced at Sierra's chest then refocused on her eyes--"Hawkins."

"It's Sierr . . ." The plane rumbled, jerked and took a sudden dip. She impulsively grabbed the arm of her gallant rescuer still seated next to her.

"Are you sure you're okay?" He leaned in to inspect her wound more closely, but when Sierra dropped her grip and pulled away, he refrained.

"We'll be landing in Pearl Harbor soon so we'd best get our gear together. It sounds like we'll have our hands full the moment we step off the plane." He stood, ambled toward the cargo door of the antique aircraft.

Surely Sierra was dreaming, hallucinating maybe, or drifting through a comatose haze conjured from the canyons of her mind. Stunned at the illusory scene her deceitful eyes portrayed, she analyzed every detail, her mind desperate to apply some sense of logic to her impossible situation.

Nurse Hawkins, why did the CO call her Nurse Hawkins? Sierra's hand drifted to her chest and grazed the brass tag that dangled from a chain around her neck. She picked up the dog tag, read the inscription: Elizabeth A. Hawkins, 1st Lt. 31298347, Hester Hawkins, 37 Harlem St, Dorchester Mass.

"Elizabeth Hawkins?" She stood, wandered toward the tail, grabbing ahold of bars on the fuselage to steady herself. "Excuse me, Sir. What kind of a craft is this?"

"It's Will, Nurse Hawkins, Dr. William--" The blare of the engines intensified as the landing gear dropped.

"Elizabeth," she muttered softly. "Call me Elizabeth." Sierra wasn't sure why she blurted out the name on her dog tag, but Elizabeth flowed from her lips before she had chance to think.

"Well, Elizabeth, this little lady is a Douglas C-47 cargo." He smiled then looked at her with concern in his eyes. "Are you sure you're okay? The shell of this heap is rock solid and you hit your head damn hard. Frankly, I was surprised you weren't knocked out."

"I'm okay, truly I am." Sierra was far from okay, but physically intact. She glanced at her clothing, a dark military garb with a US emblem on the lapel. Air force fatigues, she thought, still trying to process what happened to her, how she'd transported from a 767 to an antiquated C-47 and assumed a fictitious name in the process, all within a matter of moments--according to her recollection anyway.

As the captain approached his destination, she peered out a rectangular window still expecting to see Honolulu Airport, but the panorama displayed the burning remains of a decimated war zone. Black smoke belched from the harbor where dozens of ships, some scarcely afloat, clung to the surface consumed in a sweltering blaze.

Pearl Harbor? Will said they were approaching Pearl Harbor. But the site before her was utter devastation.

She turned toward Will. "What's today's date?" Her body writhed with a feeling of dread.

"December 7th." He furrowed his brow.

"December 7, 19--"

"41--he completed her sentence--now unless you're ready to hit the silk, I suggest you buckle in." He pointed his chin toward some empty seats. "We're starting our descent."

Sierra drifted toward the bench, slipped into the shoulder strap and buckled the belt as if she had gone through the motions hundreds of times before. But her mind was in a haze.

Pearl Harbor, December 7, 1941, a date that will live in infamy...she recalled Franklin Delano Roosevelt's address. It was the event that catapulted the United States into World War II. A chill washed over her, clenched her spine then burrowed into the pit of her stomach. Impossible. She had to be dreaming.

The sudden jolt as the aircraft landed brought her back to the moment, but she sat motionless, an icy glare frozen across her pallid face while a flurry of activity surrounded her. The platoon grabbed their gear and swarmed toward the opening hatch.

The CO flung a helmet into Sierra's lap. "Let's go, Hawkins. No time for daydreaming. The Japs virtually obliterated the entire pacific fleet." He fastened his helmet. "You winged angels signed up for combat. Well, here it is." He turned toward the rest of the crew. "Let's go ...go ...go."

Sierra's azure eyes connected with the deep brown velvet of Will's and without forethought she sprung into action. There would be time to figure out her bizarre situation later. Right now she needed to focus on the thousands of casualties that lay beyond that door. She grabbed a first aide duffle bag and took her place in line behind the other soldiers.

As she disembarked, the stench of burnt flesh overcame her. Death cries hung on the breeze. The harbor was completely decimated. Burn victims, splattered with shrapnel scattered across the setting. Chards of metal and fuselage floated on the oil-drenched water. Torpedoes and bombs had ripped through the skin of eight battleships, three cruisers, three destroyers, and several other smaller ships. Buildings lay in ruin, while flames spit through shrouds of dense, black smoke-clouds.

The bombers rained down on the unsuspecting fleet for two hours and left in their wake thousands of casualties. Patients Sierra thought, patients who needed her skill and expertise.

"We'll need a triage station," she said to Will as she rumbled through the first aide supplies. "Let's set up over there." She pointed her chin to a clearing. "Can you organize the nurses? They can tag the victims according to three categories: those who are likely to live regardless of what care they receive, those who are likely to die, regardless of what we do, and those for whom immediate care could make a positive difference in their condition.

"Yes sir, I mean ma'am." He saluted her. "Good grief, Elizabeth Hawkins, when the going gets rough, you grab the reins."

Sierra offered a timid smile. "I'm sorry Doctor, I didn't mean to take over your job. I don't know what came over me." That wasn't true. Sierra's instincts took control as they always had, especially in emergency situations. She never faltered or hesitated with any procedure and knew precisely what needed to be done. But Elizabeth Hawkins was a nurse, and in 1941 a nurse's skills were limited.

"I'm not complaining, just very impressed. Your instructions were brilliant." Will dropped his duffel beside him, glanced at his wristwatch. "It's almost noon. The hospital already has more casualties than they can handle. Let's triage here. Once the transportable patients are stable, we'll have someone move the stretchers to appropriately marked destinations."

The medic crew worked relentlessly through the afternoon with heroic valor, unaware that the Pearl Harbor attack was over. To everyone's minds, with the exception of Sierra's of course, a third wave could explode on the horizon at any moment. But Sierra had her own fears gnawing at the back of her mind. She knew her own identity beyond a shadow of a doubt and yet, on some level, Elizabeth's character, her knowledge, skills and even her memories began to creep into Sierra, mingle with her own more-and-more as the day wore on until she could scarcely distinguish the fading line between the two personalities.

And then there was Will. He and Sierra worked hand-in-hand all afternoon. She sensed his amazement at her unique skill as he watched her perform unprecedented procedures. He learned quickly too, absorbing her know-how with fastidious accuracy. But medical prowess aside, something else brewed between them, a connection, a heat and Sierra wasn't sure if the pull came from herself or Elizabeth.

"Liz, quick...over here." Will knelt beside a wounded officer.

When she approached, Sierra froze. The man, his battered body drenched in blood, lay on his side, with a huge iron rod piercing into his chest through his back and into the ground literally nailing him into the landscape.

"He's a General," Will whispered reaching for the splintered shaft.

"No, don't pull it out." She stooped beside the man, felt his faint pulse.

"He'll die. We have to pull that thing out and suture him up."

"No, Will," she insisted. "You remove that piece of metal and he will bleed out in a matter of minutes."

"Then what do you suggest?" He wiped his brow with his sleeve. "We can't just tag a general and leave him. We have to do something."

Sierra inspected the wound closely, noted the entry point, trajectory and exit then motioned for a stretcher. "I think I can save him."

Liz, I've seen you do some impressive procedures today"--he paused, gripped her arm--"but this isn't a dogface or a civi, you're talking about using a three-star General as a guinea pig."

"With your help I can do this--but you'll have to trust me." She grabbed the scissors from the duffel and began to cut away the General's uniform. "Please, Will. Let me save this man's life."

His lips flattened. "If we move him to the Pearl Harbor Hospital or that infirmary ship ...Solace, they'll never let you perform surgery." He shot a glance at the aircraft then nodded. "Okay. Let's move him into the Skytrain, lock the hatch until we're through."

The surgery lasted for hours. But despite the less than sanitary conditions, limited antiquated equipment, and lack of any advanced surgical tools, the three surgeons, Sierra, Will and Liz, performed a major miracle. Sierra's extraordinary proficiency and knowledge set the bar; Will provided a steady hand and surgery experience while Elizabeth's skill with inadequate conditions made the impossible, possible.

Together, they intubated, cut through the general's back to repair the nicked heart and lung, delicately removed the iron rod and some random shrapnel then repaired the damage to his chest. Barring infection, his prognosis was good.

After the operation, Sierra glanced at the general's dog tag before draping it back around his neck. General Robert James Walters. She hadn't even known the man's name, but she'd saved his life. Now they could move him to Pearl Harbor Hospital where he would get the post-surgery care he needed.

Will collapsed into a cushioned seat. "You scared the bejesus out of me with some of the techniques you used, but you did it, Liz. I don't know how, but you saved that general's life."

Sierra shot a look of disapproval into Will's deep green eyes, then sat beside him. "We saved him. I couldn't have performed the surgery without you."

"Well, I don't know where you learned those techniques, but what we did was nothing short of miraculous." He draped his arm over the back of her seat, slipped his hand onto her shoulder and gave it an affectionate squeezed. "You are an amazing woman, Miss Hawkins."

A soft smile crept over her face, followed by a warm tingle that floated down her spine and found refuge just below her abdomen. Thrown into the pits of hell, she froze her emotion, pushed it down so she could deal with the unconscionable situation.

Outside, what was once a paradise laid in ruin, surrounded by death and the obliteration of war, yet Sierra never felt more alive, as if the culmination of her education, her entire career and perhaps her life brought her to this place, this time, this man.

"Penny for your thoughts," Will said casually slipping his arm around her.

"What, only a penny?" she teased.

"Tough economy, and I'm a working man." He pulled her close in a pleasant one-armed hug.

For a brief few moments, cocooned inside the cargo plane, they were separated from the casualties and devastation. The war-torn world beyond the fuselage faded. Sierra quivered as the tension drained from her muscles, as if his very touch released years of pent-up stress. A rush of pure emotion released, spilled from its tethered depths, and funneled into a surge of intimate desire, a feeling she sensed was reciprocated.

Will stroked her cheek with his crooked finger then placed it under her chin. When he turned her face so their eyes met, she felt lost in his gaze. His warm breath so close she could almost taste him, she yearned for him to take her into his arms and ravage her.

Instead, he spoke to her soul without saying a word and she knew he wanted to kiss her. She nodded, and his hand immediately slid beneath her hair and drew her closer. He closed his eyes, pressed his lips over hers. She melted into his embrace. With that one blissful kiss, Will owned her.

She wasn't sure if the pounding came from her heart or his, but the forceful beating intensified until it broke her trance. Will pulled away, tucked a strand of her long sable hair behind one ear. "I guess someone has discovered us."

The beating on the hatch could no longer be ignored. "Open up in there." The voice, laced with annoyance paused before administering a few more whacks. "We have a dozen stretchers out here to load up. Let's go."

"We better get back to the team before they report us AWOL." Will aimed his head toward the general. "And we need to transport our patient to the hospital too."

By 10:00 pm, the team had treated hundreds of injured victims, many pulled from the water drenched in oil from the downed ships. The mortalities were transferred to the pathologist for identification. After treatment, patients were released or transported to various sick bays, hospitals and dispensaries in the Pearl Harbor area. Several burn cases were loaded onto the C-47 Skytrain to be flown to the Naval Hospital.

Exhausted, Sierra strapped herself into the seat next to Will and ruminated over the day's events. She had no idea how she slipped through time to the Pearl Harbor disaster, but the day changed her somehow. She'd felt a shift. It wasn't about saving General Walters.

Though gratifying, she'd felt the same rush when she'd revived a homeless woman or a newborn child. Every life had purpose regardless of their status. No, the feeling came from Elizabeth Hawkins and from working along side of Will. Sierra saw the world through an alternate reality and the impact touched a cord deep inside of her.

"Penny for your thoughts." Will placed his hand over hers sending a pleasant chill up her arm.

"Just thinking about how lucky we are." She leaned against his strong shoulder and snuggled into him. "I mean the devastation here was unconscionable, but the lives we affected ...we really made a difference today."

He put his arm around her, pulled her close enough to press his warm lips on her cheek. "That's what we do, it's who we are."

"Yes." Sierra closed her eyes and drifted into sleep, lulled by the soft purr of the C-47 engines.

§

A soft dinging noise stirred her from an illusory slumber.

"This is Captain Murphy. I hope you've enjoyed your flight. We are approaching Honolulu Airport and should be on the ground in about ten minutes. Please fasten your seatbelts and place your trays and seats in the upright position. The weather here is a pleasant 81 degrees and sunshine. Enjoy your stay and we hope you'll fly with us again soon."

Sierra rubbed the sleep from her eyes. A dream, she thought. It was all an elaborate dream.

"Sure glad you're okay, sweetie. The flight attendants were worried about you for a while there." The heavyset woman next to her shifted in her seat. "You hit your head on the window casing so hard when the plane hit that air pocket, it knocked you plumb out."

"I'm fine." Sierra reached for her head, felt the protruding lump. "It's just a little bump, nothing to be alarmed about."

"Well honey, if I was you I'd sue the airline. No telling what residual affects you might have." She snorted. "Probably at least a concussion. I'm just sayin'."

"Thank you for your concern ma'am, but it's really nothing." Sierra pulled up the shade on her window and peered out to watch the final descent. When the plane landed she waited until all the passengers disembarked then grabbed her things from the overhead compartment. As she headed down the aisle the flight attendant called to her.

"Miss, is this yours?" She held out her hand to reveal a tiny gold charm. "It was on the seat of 3-A. That's where you were sitting, weren't you?"

"Yes, but I don't think I--" She stopped midsentence when she realized what the flight attendant was holding. It was a lapel pin, the letters US. Sierra trembled remembering where she saw the gold emblem. How was it possible? Had she really been transported back to 1941? She took the pin, slipped it into her pocket, thanking the attendant.

Something happened on that flight from Atlanta to Honolulu. She was at Pearl Harbor. She could still taste the stench of death and decimation, still felt a lingering tingle on her lips where Will kissed her. She drew her hand to her mouth. Whatever occurred was real and she wouldn't let it remain a mystery.

As soon as she got to the gate, she sat down, pulled out her IPad, and Googled the attack on Pearl Harbor. Sifting through a slideshow of pictures already seared in her mind, she shook her head. There was no way she could have dreamed such vivid images of the disaster--unless she was there...but how? A chill raised the hairs on her neck and surged down her back.

She slipped her IPad into its case and headed for the baggage claim. By the time Sierra reached her flight's carousel, only one forlorn bag remained. She grabbed her suitcase, hailed a cab.

"Aloha." The cabbie reached for her luggage. "Where to Miss?

"Royal Hawaiian, Waikiki, please."

"I'll take that." The oddly familiar voice hailed from behind her.

Sierra spun around. A dazed look washed over her face. Will?

"Dr. Norton. It's so nice to see you again." He switched her bag to his left hand and stretched his right to greet her. "Trent McArthur at your service. You didn't think I'd leave you to a taxi service, did you?"

Stunned at the resemblance between the man in front of her and Will, she stumbled over her words. "No ...yes, I mean, it's nice to see you again, Mr. McArthur." She reached out, clenched and shook his hand.

"Please, call me Trent. My car is parked just over there." He tilted his head toward a close by lot. "I will never be able to thank you enough for flying out here. Brooklyn is thrilled. I could see the fear drain from her little face when I told her you were on your way."

"I reviewed her files on the flight." She nonchalantly gazed back at Trent McArthur, still dumbstruck that she hadn't remembered what he looked like, and how the vivid, intimate feelings she felt toward Will somehow shifted to Trent. The likeness was uncanny.

"And . . ." He stopped and turned toward her, his eyes shot into hers and his face went pale.

"Oh, don't worry." She assured him, switching into doctor mode. "I agree with her physicians regarding her infection. But there is a new drug I'd like to try. The success rate has been phenomenal."

Mr. McArthur stood silent, his stare boring into her and she could swear he felt the same familiarity. Not like an old acquaintance, but rather like they shared an intimate secret.

"If you have a problem with a drug, I can treat her with something else. It's just that I think Brooklyn is a prime candidate for--"

"No." He paused a beat before continuing. "I completely trust your assessment of her condition and will agree to any course of treatment you deem necessary."

He opened the door and helped her into his car, threw the suitcase in the backseat. Sliding in next to her he asked, "Did you enjoy your flight?"

"Yes. We hit a pretty big storm at one point with a good bit of turbulence, but overall, the trip was fine." Envisioning the side trip to Pearl Harbor, she repositioned herself.

"Good." He placed his arm on the back of her seat then looked over his shoulder to back out of his parking space.

Pulling his hand back, he grazed Sierra's arm and sent a shot of electricity through her. She turned her head to peer out her window, closed her eyes until the sensation eased. What happened to her today--what was happening to her now? Sierra was a highly intelligent woman, a surgeon.

How could she have flashes of another time, and desire for someone she barely knew? The connection she'd felt from the moment she'd touched McArthur's little girl confused her, but now? The bond that flowed between her and this family overwhelmed her with incredible emotion, the likes of which she had never known. They weren't like the highs she'd experienced after an intense surgery. Something mystical tied her to the McArthur family.

"I know you must be exhausted, Dr. Norton, and I'll drop you off at your hotel if you prefer, but I know a little girl laying in a hospital bed that would love to see you, if you're up for it." Trent glanced at her, his eyebrows raised.

"I slept on the flight, Mr. McArthur."

He held up his hand in objection. "Please, it's Trent."

An amenable smile lit her face. "Trent. And you can call me Sierra." She turned her attention to the scenery to avoid eye contact with him in hopes to reduce the intense attraction she was feeling. "Let's go to the hospital. I'm anxious to see Brooklyn too, and I'd like to get her started on the medication as soon as possible. I can't promise anything, but with any luck, we'll have her home in a couple of days."

"That's the best news I've heard in months."

When they opened the door to Brook's room, she sat upright. "Sera," she said with a fragile voice. "I knew you'd come."

"You did?" Sierra brushed the stray blond hairs from her face and sat on the bedside next to her. "And how did you know that? I live awfully far from you now."

"I know, but Mommy said you'd come."

Trent leaned over and whispered in Sierra's ear. "Sorry I forgot to mention that. Brooklyn insists that her mother visits her from heaven."

His warm breath sent a tingle down her neck, she breathed in deeply to avoid a visible reaction, and focused on Brooklyn. "Well, your mommy was right. I'm here." Sierra's lips flattened. "And we're going to make you all better, okay?"

"I know. Mommy told me that too." The child reached her hand toward Sierra, dragging the IV stuck in her frail little arm along with it, squeezed her fingers tightly around Sierra's thumb. "Everything will be alright now." She leaned back against her pillow and closed her eyes, still clinging to her doctor.

When Brooklyn fell asleep, Sierra consulted with the medical team and started the little girl on a new regiment of medications.

"Is it normal for children to pretend to talk to someone they've lost?" Trent asked Sierra with a tone of concern.

"A lot of children create imaginary friends." Sierra replied. "Your daughter has been through hell and back. If talking to her mother gives her some comfort, then more power to her. Besides, whose to say she isn't really communicating with Alyssa?"

"Really?" he protested. "You're a doctor, a scientist. The last thing I ever expected was to hear you advocate supernatural manifestations."

"I'm not advocating anything, but stranger things have happened." After her brush with time travel, far be it from her to question Brooklyn's connection with the afterlife.

Trent's analysis of Sierra, though spot on, couldn't explain the mystical force weaving their lives together. Throughout the ride to the Royal Hawaiian hotel, Sierra mused over the source of the odd occurrences. Maybe Brooklyn was right. Perhaps her mother was orchestrating the whole stream of events from beyond the grave. Something supernatural certainly twisted Sierra thoughts into believing she actually visited Pearl Harbor during the onset of World War II.

The faint whispers of Franklin Delano Roosevelt's words drifted through her mind, "We have nothing to fear but fear itself." Sierra was not afraid. But the lingering echo of her visit to the past haunted her. She hadn't been dreaming or conjured a vision of a past life. Had she? And the resemblance between Will and Trent baffled her. She hadn't felt a connection to him the first time they'd met. Why now? Why did it all happen and what did it mean?

"Here we are." Trent pulled into the circular entrance of the hotel and idled the car. A bellhop appeared immediately, opened Sierra's door. She started to get out, but Trent gently grabbed her arm. "I can't thank you enough for flying out here to treat my daughter."

Her heart skipped a beat at his touch. "You're welcome," she managed to mutter then paused, searching his hazel eyes. "Brooklyn is a very special little girl." Against her wishful instincts, she turned and disappeared into the lobby.

§

The third day into the new drug regiment, Brook's cheeks glowed with color. Her appetite returned and by all indications, the infection was subsiding.

"You're a miracle worker, Dr. Norton." Trent picked up his little girl, now free from IVs and wires, and squeezed her close to him.

"She's not a hundred percent yet, but she's out of the woods." Sierra felt a rush of emotion as she watched the two of them hug. She touched Brook's back, rubbed it softly. "Would you like to go home and sleep in your own bed tonight?" she asked the child.

"Yes. Oh yes, Sera." The little girl turned, leaned toward Sierra and rubbed her cheek. "See, I told you everything would be alright." She giggled and reached her arms around both the adults, pulling the threesome together.

"I guess my job here is done." Sierra reluctantly pulled away. "I should be getting back to Atlanta."

"Sierra," Trent paused a beat. "I'll never be able to repay you for--"

She interrupted him, "You already have. Just seeing the smile on her face is payment enough."

He slid the child on his hip. "At least let me treat you to dinner. Better yet, let me cook for you tonight. I've become quite a gourmet chef since I've become Mr. Mom for this little one."

"Oh please, Sera. Come have dinner." Brooklyn chimed in. "You can have a sleepover too." The child looked at Trent. "Can't she daddy?"

He raised an eyebrow and shrugged. "Out of the mouths of babes." He chuckled. "I think dinner will do for now, missy." He swished his forefinger down her button nose.

"Dinner would be lovely." Sierra smiled. "What time shall I be there?"

"Now would work for us." He tickled his daughter's tummy. "Right sweetie?"

Brooklyn clapped her hands together with an ear-to-ear grin. "Now, now."

"I think a relaxing afternoon would be good for all of us," Sierra agreed. "And I'm sure Brook is ready leave this place."

The little girl nodded her head up-and-down then snuggled into her daddy.

§

Sierra couldn't remember the last time she'd had such a pleasant afternoon. Brooklyn took great pleasure in showing off her stuffed animals and dollies but, still weak from fighting the infection, she was quite content to snuggle between Sierra and her daddy while they took turns reading stories to her. When she finally fell asleep Trent took her up stairs to tuck her in bed.

Stacking Brooklyn's books on the coffee table, Sierra noticed an old scrapbook and began to leaf through the worn pages. Faded newspaper clippings and photographs, yellowed with age, showed the highlights of a lost generation.

What a wonderful family heirloom, Sierra thought. She knew very little about her roots, had only a few pictures of her mother and father. Both absorbed in their own career, they had a little time for fluff, and as an only child she'd felt closer to her nanny than her own parents.

As Sierra turned the brittle page, her face went pale. "Will," she whispered. Glaring at the aged news clipping, she inspected the picture more closely. There was no doubt in her mind, the man in the photo was Will dressed in his military fatigues and standing next to a striking woman, directly in front of a Douglas C-47 cargo Skytrain.

"Penny for your thoughts," Trent said as he strolled down the stairway.

Startled, Sierra sat up with a jolt and clutched her hand to her heart. "Oh my gosh," she said. "You scared the bejesus out of me."

"I haven't heard that phrase since my grandfather passed away." Trent sat down beside her, glanced at the picture that had Sierra so engrossed. "That's Gramps, right there." He pointed at Will. "William Trenton McArthur. I was named after him."

Sierra's mouth fell open. "This man, William McArthur was your grandfather?"

"Sure was. That picture was taken just after the Japanese bombed Pearl Harbor, the day he met Gram." He pointed to the woman in the photograph. "That's my grandmother, Elizabeth Hawkins McArthur, but Gramps called her Liz."

Completely stunned, Sierra glared at the picture of Elizabeth Hawkins. She didn't recognize her, and yet somehow she knew the woman from the inside out. Trent continued pointing out news clippings and describing the cast of characters, but Sierra was caught in a cyclone of memories swirling back-and-forth between 1941 and 2014.

What she experienced was scientifically impossible. And Trent was Will's grandson? The kiss that still lingered on Sierra's lips had ignited a romance without which Brooklyn and her father would've never been born. Was that what her time slip to Pearl Harbor was all about?

"And this is General Robert James Walters..." The muted echo of Will's voice intermingled with Trent's until the two melded into one.

He drew his hand back and grazed Sierra's wrist sending a warm tingle up her arm to the base of her neck. "I'm sorry, what did you say?" she asked.

"General Walters, he single-handedly saved an entire battalion, over 1000 soldiers, when he sneaked behind enemy lines and procured German plans staging a massive attack in southern Italy." Trent radiated pride. "My grandparents saved his life at Pearl Harbor three years earlier. If it wasn't for William McArthur and Elizabeth Hawkins, over 1000 soldiers would have died that day."

And icy chill trickle down Sierra's back. If she hadn't been ripped back to 1941 the General would've died, and all of those soldiers would've perished along with him because he wouldn't have been there to save them.

Her first impulse was elation, she wanted to tell Trent that she performed the surgery, she removed the rod piercing through the general's chest, "Yes, but I..." she halted, realizing how absurd her affirmation would sound. And when she thought about it, she didn't want to take credit for saving General Walters. Will and Elizabeth performed the surgery. Only Sierra's consciousness, her expertise, assisted them.

"You what?" he asked.

"I...think that's an incredible story, Trent. Will and Liz were truly heroes. Sierra eyes shifted from the scrapbook to the man sitting in front of her. When their gaze connected, she saw a brief image of Will fade into his grandson's face. But it was Trent's velvet-brown eyes that mesmerized her. For a long moment they shared an enigmatic stare, as if lost in each other.

He squinted, touched her hand. "I know this is going to sound like a line or completely ridiculous, but I can't shake the feeling that we've done this before ...in another place or time."

Her fingers wrapped around his. "Perhaps we have." A soft smile emerged that grew across her face.

"Maybe you should stay for a few days longer." He paused a beat still drinking in her eyes. "For Brooklyn."

"I--" His mouth over covered hers, extinguishing her reply. She melted into him. With that one blissful kiss, Trent owned her.

§

The soft shimmer of three translucent images glimmered on the stairway, unnoticed by Trent and Sierra. Only Brooklyn, who stood at the top of the steps, delighted in the flicker of their presence.

"We did it." Alyssa beamed.

Liz draped her arm around Brooklyn's mother, "It is their destiny to be together."

"Sierra is a wonderful woman and we owe her so much." Will took Elizabeth's hand. "I think our work is done here. It's time for us to go."

Liz kissed Alyssa's cheek. "Your destiny awaits." Smiling, she turned, took Will's hand and they spun into a sparkling swirl of light before dissolving into a glittery mist that faded into the night.

Alyssa held out her hand to Brooklyn. "And you need to get back to bed, dear one." She whirled around her daughter cocooning the child with the warmth of her glow. "Everything is as it should be now." She kissed her daughter's forehead. "Take care of your daddy and remember, I am always with you." She placed the child back into her bed then shimmered into the soft glow of the night-light.

Moments later Sierra tiptoed up the stairs to check on the little girl. She stood by the side of Brooklyn's bed, felt for any lingering fever then leaned down and kissed her cheek. The night-light flickered, dimmed. Sierra never noticed the soft shimmer that drifted from the light across the shadows of the darkened room then nestled into her heart. Brook opened her eyes and tiny slit.

"Good night, Sera."

"Sweet dreams, dear one," Sierra whispered.

The Pegasus Chronicle

Book Five

Casi McLean

The Pegasus Chronicle

Katlyn Harris leveled the corner of the mysterious painting she'd hung above the hearth. Still captivated by its mysterious allure, she stared deep into the canvas. The figure, barely noticeable at first, blended into the background. An afterthought perhaps, a minor element nestled within the landscape to evoke intrigue like the twists she'd plotted in her manuscripts. But once she brushed away the cobwebs, blew off years of powdery dust, his image captivated her.

"Collin," she whispered. She'd recognize him anywhere--the man who came to her in dreams for as long as she could remember. Katlyn knew him intimately. She'd memorized every detail of his strong, handsome face. From the moment she'd discovered the dusty picture hidden behind a trunk in the attic, his image mesmerized her, beckoned her by day and tantalized her dreams at night.

She strolled toward the kitchen, poured her third cup of coffee then glanced at her watch. Jake would be arriving with the rest of her things soon. She was so ready to sleep in her own bed again. Yet the soft lapping of the lake beyond the trees soothed her at night.

Here, she listened to the silence, relaxed to the tranquil hush of unfamiliar stillness. She'd almost forgotten the comforting whir of a cricket's chirp and the soft rustling of squirrels scurrying through the forest. The bustling city traffic lulled her to sleep for so many years, humming like white noise, but the quiet here comforted her, wrapped her in a blanket of silent serenity.

Cupping her hands around the steamy mug, she drew it closer, inhaled the rich aroma before sipping the hot, nutty brew then walked back to the parlor. Inheriting her aunt's home was a Godsend. Not that she delighted in losing her only living relative--a woman she never even knew existed-- but the failing economy destroyed Katlyn's livelihood.

When the Washington Herald closed its doors, her column hadn't been picked up; and despite making the New York Times Best Seller list, The Pegasus Chronicle had yet to bring in the kind of royalties she needed to survive. Her meager savings lasted less than a year, and the $100K equity she'd accrued through almost a decade of mortgage payments simply evaporated. If it hadn't been for Aunt Kathrin's will and this rickety old Victorian house Katlyn inherited, her life would have spiraled downward.

She'd never envisioned herself living on a secluded cove in the middle of nowhere, but after only a few weeks she'd begun to feel at home here, safe despite the solitude. Rummaging through the old place distracted her from the misfortune, and unraveling the mystery of a reclusive relative rekindled her creative soul.

Glancing at the painting again, she felt her heart race. She knew every curve of Collin's face. Night after night he came to her, enchanted her with his sensuous smile and charismatic charm. The artist captured the morning sun dancing across his face and the shimmer in those mesmeric blue eyes. But why did he look so forlorn?

Placing her coffee cup on the mantel, she softly touched the landscape. The clearing behind her house had aged. Trees had grown taller and the underbrush flourished with dense overgrowth now, but the site was unmistakable. Every day for the past two weeks she'd walked down to the lake, sat on the same stone bench, gazed across the glistening water. The sandy shoreline hadn't changed.

Katlyn ran her fingers across the timeworn canvas, stopping for a moment on the obscure figure. Despite the vague brush strokes, she felt his cobalt eyes entice her. All those years she'd thought him only a figment of her imagination, an imaginary friend to help her through her fears.

How thrilling to discover that Collin hadn't been a mere creation of her childhood dreams. Kathrin must have known him. Perhaps she'd tucked away some pictures amongst her belongings, something that would shed some light on who he was, or why Katlyn felt so connected to him. The corners of her mouth curled upward.

All her life Kat had felt discarded. She had no family, no one who cared. Kathrin's Will changed everything. But there were still so many unanswered questions. What did the woman look like? Why was her existence kept a secret? And how did she die? The lawyers told Kat nothing and, though she'd ordered the death certificate, she'd yet to receive it. Kat knew nothing about her reclusive aunt. Why did the woman leave all her worldly possessions to a niece she never even met?

The shrill doorbell ring broke the utter silence, jolting Katlyn from her musings. Her heart pounding, she grasped at her chest. "Jake," she whispered then scurried toward the entryway. The clunking of her heels against the hardwood floors echoed through the scantly furnished room. She peeked through the beveled-glass window, flung open the door.

"Jacob Morgan, you scared me half to death." Smiling, she hugged the young man. "I'm so glad you're here. Please, come in."

"I thought you were expecting me." He granted a wry grin, raising an eyebrow. "But I have to admit I've been known to have a startling affect on women."

Katlyn simpered. "Right ...I was totally absorbed in another world. This house is fabulous." She grabbed Jake's hand. "Come on. I have to show you something." Pulling him inside, she dragged him into the parlor, stopping directly in front of the fireplace. "Isn't it amazing?"

"Typical 1950's architecture, dramatic stacked stone, but I wouldn't call it amazing."

"No, not the hearth." She laughed, pointed above the mantel. "The painting. Isn't it absolutely fabulous? I found it in the attic under layers of dust, but once I cleaned it up . . ." She stared so deep into the landscape she could almost smell the less green foliage. "There's something about this picture that totally fascinates me."

"I can see that. I guess it's nice. But a sad little man sitting alone on a bench by a lake doesn't really excite me." He spun toward Katlyn, picked her up and swung her around. "You, on the other hand..." He kissed her on the cheek before setting her down again. "You look great, Kat. This place must agree with you."

"Typical male response." She rolled her eyes, shook her head. "Well, maybe you'll appreciate my exquisite picture more once you see the place. You ready for the grand tour?"

"Wait a second. Stand over there by the hearth and let me get a quick picture of you first. Something to say for posterity." He teased, flipped out his smart-phone and snapped a shot before she had a chance to protest.

Hands on her hips, with her head tilted slightly to the right, she smiled a cute, pouty grin.

"Perfect." He beamed, admiring his photographic prowess. He stuffed the phone into his back pocket.

"Can I show you around now?" She raised her eyebrows, crooked her forefinger indicating he should follow her.

"Absolutely." He nodded.

Katlyn moved room-to-room with Jake in tow, babbling on about each amazing nook and treasured knick-knack. When they finally reached the attic, she pointed out where she'd found her mysterious painting, before leading him to the window seat. They sat for a while, chatting and gazing across the back of the property overlooking the lake.

"Thanks again for hauling the rest of my stuff to Atlanta, Jake. There's no way I could have made this move without you," she said in earnest glancing at him. "I'm so glad you're staying a few days to help me get settled."

"That's what friends do." He nudged her shoulder. "And God knows I've earned the vacation time. So, it sounds like you like living here."

"I love the house. It's beautiful and peaceful, but..."

"But what?" Shifting his position, he leaned against the side of the window seat so he could look into her face.

"Lake Lanier is a lot farther north of Atlanta than I thought and it's so far from D.C."

He tucked a strand of long golden hair behind her left ear. "You'll be fine, Kat." His eyes burned with sincerity. "Things happen for a reason. I have a feeling this move will be the best thing that ever happened to you."

"But I'll miss you--miss everyone so much." She looked down at the floor and kicked at a dust bunny. "Maybe I should have just sold the old place."

"Hey." Jake lifted her chin, looked deep into her eyes. "What happened to the bubbling excitement you've had since you found out you owned this place--the years of writing material it will provide? Besides, you make friends easier than anyone I know."

"I guess." She turned her head to gaze out the window again. "But I've been here two weeks and haven't met a soul yet."

"I see." Jake leaned back against the side panel. "And just how much time have you spent away from this house?"

"I went to the store for groceries the first day." She smirked. "Does that count?"

"Hardly, but now that I'm here that will change." Standing, Jake offered his hand, pulled her up. "Okay, first things first, let's get you settled. Once we get this place feeling more like your home, we'll go investigate the area and meet some of the locals." He draped his arm around her shoulders then led her downstairs. "I promise I'll stay with you until you're happy, deal?"

"Deal," she purred.

As much as Kat would have loved to fall for Jake, their relationship never went in that direction. She felt close to him, loved him, but not romantically, and he felt the same way. Jake was like the brother she'd never had. It seemed odd when she thought about it.

With his tall athletic stature, sandy blond hair and violet eyes, Jake was the image of her soul mate, the man she'd dreamed of her whole life. And his honesty stood nothing short of remarkable in this day and age—like a throwback to a simpler era before the me-society replaced integrity. She knew he'd keep his promise, but it would be hard to watch him drive back to D.C., regardless of how long he stayed.

By the time the two friends unpacked everything from the truck it was nearly dinnertime. Katlyn's bed and kitchen table was set in place and the boxes were empty, the contents tucked neatly away.

Selling the bulk of her furniture, clothing and trinkets at a massive garage sale was a brilliant idea. It put cash in her pocket and left fewer items to haul across four states. Only absolute necessities and some treasured possessions with sentimental value made the move.

Jake hauled the empty boxes out to the street then washed his hands in the kitchen sink. Noticing the keys to Katlyn's Miata on the windowsill, he grabbed them before strolling into the parlor.

"So, are you going to feed me, or do I get to take you out for an authentic southern meal?"

"Unless you're up for scrambled eggs, I think we'll be dining out." She pulled a clip from her hair, releasing thick blonde locks that curled over her shoulders and spilled down to her waist. "I'm starving, but I have no idea where to eat. Dahlonega isn't far though. We can head in that direction. I'm sure we'll run across something along the way."

Placing her clip on the mantel, she glanced at the painting again. A silvery haze hung over the lagoon as twilight approached. But this morning hadn't she seen glints of morning sunlight reflecting in Collin's eyes?

"You coming?" Jake shook the keys to draw her attention, held them out to her.

She turned toward the front door. "Yes ...I just thought . . ." Gazing back over her shoulder, she felt a chill run down her back.

"Thought what? Are you okay, Kat?"

"Yeah." She shuddered, looked at Jake's smile and her perplexed feeling melted away. "You drive. I think I'm more exhausted than I thought I was."

The rolling foothills of north Georgia reminded Katlyn of the view along Skyline Drive near the base of the Blue Ridge Mountains. She could tell that maneuvering the winding roads in her little Miata gave Jake a sense of nirvana. A tranquil expression splashed across his face as he gripped the steering wheel tightly, pressed down on the accelerator around each curve and leaned into the swerves.

Katlyn cracked an endearing smile, then gazed across the breathtaking panorama. Brilliant colors blanketed the mid-October countryside, now softened by the evening sun. In the distance, drifting clouds hovered below a mountainous skyline and a silvery mist loomed above the silent vale. Kat could almost feel it beckon her.

The fog lifted as they approached, revealing a spray of twinkling lights intermingled with neon fireflies pirouetting above a flashing sign appropriately read Facetious Fireflies.

"Look, Kat, it's a carnival." He veered off the road, pulling onto a grass parking lot then breathed in deeply.

"Ahhh, I haven't smelled that since I was a little boy."

Katlyn took a deep breath, closed her eyes. "Hot dogs, burgers, cotton candy, funnel cakes ...it may not be the healthiest meal in town, but it could be fun. What do you think?"

"Let's do it." Jake jumped over the side of the Miata, walked around to open the door for Kat.

A heavily trodden gravel path wound throughout the park, crossing at the midway. After a brief pit stop for hotdogs and fries, they strolled around the grounds. Kat's eyes gleamed as she drank in the ambiance. How long had it been since she'd spent time at a carnival? She used to love the sideshows and games, but her favorite activity and always been riding the Ferris wheel.

Jake indulged her, insisting they ride everything, but saving the carousel for last.

"So what's so exciting about a merry-go-round?" Katlyn nudged her friend, leaning into him.

"It's not just a merry-go-round. It's a carousel, complete with rings."

"Rings?" Her eyes narrowed into an inquisitive stare.

"You mean to tell me you've never heard the phrase 'catch the brass ring'?"

"I suppose I have, but I didn't know it had anything to do with a carousel?"

Jake shook his head. "A writer, and you've never heard of carousel rings? The old legend says when you catch the brass ring on a carousel ride your dreams come true."

"Right, I'm sure cosmetic karma bursts through the clouds to bestow wonderful gifts upon you." Katlyn rolled her eyes.

"I don't think that was actually the premise. But in the early 20th-century carousels held more than just a simple circular ride, they had a game of sorts, with little rings about this big." He put the tips of his forefinger and thumb together to form a circle. "They were small, hard to grasp with the horses moving up-and-down as they sped past the mechanical arm. Each time someone hooked a finger into a ring, another one slid down to replace it. And this particular carousel has rings. Come on, I'll show you."

He grabbed her hand, pulled her toward the merry-go-round, a beautifully preserved antique apparatus with flashing lights that spelled out Déjà vu.

"Okay, I see what the riders are doing, but what's the point?" Kat stared as each individual who rode an outside horse strained to reach for the little silver rings.

"The person who grabs the most rings gets a free ride."

"So they're battling to see who can get the most rings for one lousy ride?"

"Yes, but that's only part of it. The big prize is the brass ring. There's only one of those, and it rarely shows up. If you catch it, you win a stuffed animal or something." Jake leaned against the railing and watched each rider reach for the treasure. "But if you believe in the legend, catching a brass ring makes your dreams come true."

"Well, I'm not sure I have dreams anymore." Katlyn gazed past the crowd toward the attendant, an attractive man dressed in jeans and a royal blue T-shirt, wiping down the carved wooden animals. When he stepped to the side, she saw the back half of a white horse. She leaned to inspect it more closely and . . .

"What about Pegasus?" Jakes voice broke her trance, drawing her attention back to him. "It's a great story, Kat. The book should be a movie. How do you come up with such great ideas like that?"

She scrunched her facial features together, pondering his question. "I didn't really come up with it." Then, cocking her head, she grinned. "It's more like it came to me, evolved from dreams I had as a little girl. A beautiful white-winged horse whisked me away to a fantasy world. There was a little boy there and he . . ." She stopped herself mid-sentence. "I heard too many fairytales as a child, right? Anyway, the dreams inspired my book."

Jake leaned over and kissed her on the forehead. Katlyn smiled, moved slightly to the left to glance over his shoulder--and froze. The attended moved, revealing the entire body of the carved animal.

"What's wrong?" Jake spun around.

Katlyn stood speechless, staring into the nostrils of a sleek white wooden Pegasus. His eyes sparkled like fine sapphires, and she could swear she saw his wings move.

The attendant appeared without warning from behind the saddle of the animal. "Care to take a chance to have your dreams come true?"

Katlyn's gaze shot from the winged creature to the strange man. She paused a moment before answering. "I'm afraid I don't have any. At least not dreams that could actually come true, anyway."

His hypnotic eyes drew her closer, lured her forward until she could feel such an intense mystical aura that everything else faded into the background. Now, she couldn't tell if the odd sensation radiated from the mythical creature or the mysterious man, but it didn't matter. Whatever the source, she knew she had to mount the horse and ride.

"No dreams?" The man whispered to her. He pulled a ticket from his pocket, offered it to her. "And yet I sense your intrigue."

Kat mindlessly took the voucher. "It's Pegasus, every detail is . . ." She wanted to say familiar, amazing, the avatar of the winged-creature upon which she'd sailed the heavens in her dreams, but that would have sounded quite insane. Instead, she simply said, "It's so beautiful."

"Perhaps you've given up on your dreams too easily." He glared at her as if searching deep into her soul. "The horse has chosen you. And he never makes a mistake." The man held out his hand to help her aboard.

She remained motionless, still mesmerized. The intricate details etched within the horse's carved body displayed musculature so authentic it almost rippled, and the thick white mane glistened in the twinkling carousel lights. Completely enchanted, Katlyn held out her hand, strode forward.

"Kat." When Jake's voice echoed beside her, she instinctively turned to look at him, her daze disrupted.

"I take it we're riding the carousel?"

"Yes, it's such an odd coincidence, don't you think--Pegasus, I mean?" Stepping aboard the ride, she reached for Jake's hand.

"It's kismet." He smirked, hopped aboard and kissed her cheek.

After lifting Katlyn onto the back of her horse, he slid on the silver steed beside her. When the ride began, he reached over, took Kat's hand in his and squeezed it tightly. Soft music streamed from the calliope as the carousel picked up speed and the park lights blurred into a constant spray of multicolored illumination encircling the swirling platform. Kat's head began to spin. She heard Jake's voice--what was he saying?

"The ring, Kat. Catch the brass ring."

Katlyn reached as far as she could, stretching her arm, aiming her hooked forefinger directly at the gleaming brass circle perched on the mechanical arm.

But the moment she touched the golden hoop, the sky opened into a burst of fiery light. She felt Jake's hand clinging to hers then watched him dissolve into the mist below, like a fading hologram.

§

Pegasus took flight, transforming into a mighty winged-horse speeding through the mist, and the brass ring expanded into a vast halo before them, opening a portal into another world. The vision shattered reality as if all her dreams morphed into a passionate crescendo bursting into that one moment.

The azure sky shone deeper blue than Katlyn had ever seen; a brilliant sun warmed and soothed her. The experience seemed utterly impossible, extraordinary, terrifying––yet she wasn't afraid. Was she dreaming again, dying, or completely insane? She clung to the mane of her magical dream-horse, intoxicated by sheer bliss.

Pegasus flew through the clouds before slowly descending, circling as if searching for something. Gliding between the lush greenery, he softly landed, knelt, and bowed his head so Katlyn could slide from his back. Standing again, he pranced forward to gently nuzzle her, his sapphire eyes glistening in the sunlight.

"Oh my gosh." Katlyn brushed the mass of hair from her face. "That was amazing."

She had no idea what just transpired, but it was the most incredible ride she'd ever experienced. The horse shook his head back-and-forth, stomped his front hoof on the ground. So now what she wondered.

"Live your dreams," Pegasus spoke into her thoughts. "Find him."

Stunned at an answer to her unspoken question, she stared at the animal then timidly spoke. "Find who?" She glanced around, but nothing looked familiar. "Where are we?"

A wave of anxiety surged through her with every instinct inside screaming caution; this was more than a simple carousel ride. It couldn't be real, a dream perhaps, or a manifestation of childhood imagination. Perhaps she'd suffered a heart attack or a stroke. She could have slipped into a coma--or maybe she was dead. Could her winged fantasy have flown her through the gates of heaven?

"My job is done. It's your turn, Katlyn." Pegasus nuzzled her again, turned and trotted toward the forest.

"Wait." Katlyn ran after him. "You can't just leave me here in the middle of nowhere." What do I do? Where shall I go? Before her questions shifted from her thoughts to her lips, a reply drifted into her mind.

"Follow your heart." Pegasus whipped his tail, stretching his neck to the right. "Take the path through those trees. You will find your destiny." He pranced into the forest, disappearing amidst the dense foliage.

Katlyn walked toward the trees to a worn path, followed it through the woods. She heard the familiar sound of water lapping on the shore. Her heart beat faster with every step. The end of the trail opened to a clearing with a lake beyond and a small stone bench--her bench. Pegasus brought her home. But why? She sat, gazing across the lake in astonished bewilderment. What just happened? Jake, where are you?

Deep in thought, she didn't hear him approach.

"Is it really you?"

She snapped around, disconcerted.

"Who's there?" Squinting against the bright sunlight, she could see a dark figure approaching from the shadows. Jake? No, it wasn't his voice. She stood, backed away. One couldn't be too careful these days.

"Who are you? And what are you doing on my property?" She scowled at the man, hoping he'd back away. He didn't.

"Your property?" He walked closer. "I'm afraid you're a bit confused, Madam. That's my home atop the hill." He motioned toward the house and Katlyn glanced upward, shielding her eyes against the brilliant sun. What was he talking about? She'd been living in that house for two weeks now amongst Aunt Kathrin's belongings. Perhaps this man wandered further down the shoreline than he'd realized.

"It is you," he whispered.

Startled, Katlyn realized the man stood only a few feet away now. His sandy blond hair tossed slightly in the wind, and when his cobalt eyes met hers, her heart raced. She could barely breathe, could say nothing. Instead, she stood in front of him completely confused, utterly spellbound--Collin, her Collin. She knew it with every fiber inside of her, but how?

She'd acknowledged that Collin was the man in her antique painting and was convinced Kathrin knew him, but the picture must have been painted over sixty years ago. Collin couldn't be here. Not now, here in her own back yard. Could he?

Every rational bone in her body screamed that the last half hour of her life was sheer fantasy. Maybe she'd been thrown off the carousel. That's it. She'd hit her head and lost consciousness. The flight of Pegasus, her unrealistic desire for Collin...it all churned together in her mind to create a beautiful mirage, but not reality.

Collin stood in front of her now, so close she could sense the raw desire rising inside of him.

"My beautiful Kat. I've dreamed of you my whole life. And now you're here." The line of his mouth curled into a soft smile.

He reached over and with the back of his forefinger pushed a strand of her golden hair away from her eyes--the way he had so many times in her dreams. "You've finally come to me."

Touching her own face, Katlyn traced the path Collin's finger grazed. "What do you mean I've come to you?" Her voice trembled with every word.

She felt his touch as real as her own. They stood face-to-face. But if she actually saw him, she would have had to slip backward through time, which was absurd, impossible. Time travel only occurred in science fiction ...and Pegasus evolved from ancient myths. He'd manifested in the mind of a scared little girl to calm her fears. Neither really existed. Katlyn's dreams couldn't have spun her through time--could they?

"I don't understand." She stared at him, her mind battling to distinguish fantasy from reality.

"And yet you know in your heart who I am." Collin held out his hand to her. "Don't be afraid." Reaching down he grasped her hand in his.

She felt a surge of energy rush through her body and the woman within awaken.

"Come. Sit next to me." He led her to the stone bench, sat down. "We have so much to talk about."

She slid beside him. "But...how?" She stammered, still trying to make sense of what happened.

"I can't answer that, except to say that it is providence. The promise our lives would be set straight has come true. I know it seems inexplicable." He softly squeezed her hand. "But this is our destiny."

She looked deep into his eyes. "Collin, it really is you?" Reaching up to touch his cheek, she ran her fingers across his face. The face she had memorized, known her whole life. He was Collin, the boy who rode the winged-horse with her as a child, protected her, grew up with her--the man of her dreams, her soul mate.

Perhaps she slipped into a coma, a fantasy world, but Katlyn didn't care. Wherever she was, however it happened, Collin was here, sitting beside her and she could touch him, smell him, feel her desire stirring inside. She had loved him all her life, but never in her wildest dreams did she imagined she'd feel the warmth of his skin next to hers.

Collin pulled her close in a passionate embrace and pressed his soft lips over her mouth, then nibbled his way to her neck and ear. "I've loved you forever and will through eternity," he whispered.

The floodgates to Katlyn's soul released and she clung to him, kissing him with a lifetime of pent-up desire. Her body melted into his, stirring a fire deep inside, a passion so strong it defied time. She didn't know how she came to him. But it made no difference.

Collin said they were destined to be together. Perhaps that was why she'd never fallen in love, never been able to think of loving anyone else. Collin was always there, in her head, her dreams, and in her heart. She knew him better than she knew herself. And now, he sat right in front of her; nothing else mattered.

§

"The ring, Kat. Reach for the brass ring."

Jake grasped her hand firmly while she stretched her body, reaching for the sparkling loop. The lights flashed in wild frenzy, the music intensified--and his stomach turned upside-down. Trying to hold back its contents, he squeezed his eyes, drew in a deep, long breath then slowly let it out.

His head spun and he could see nothing but a blur of flashing color. Gripping the pole of his wooden steed, he tilted his head forward and leaned against it to steady himself, still clutching Kat's hand with a death grip. He wouldn't let her fall.

When the ride began to slow, Jake sat up and gazed over at her--but Kat had vanished. Instead of her hand, he clung to the tether of her white winged-horse. Turning his torso around, he searched for her. Surely the attendant would have stopped the ride if she had been flung from her mount. Had she slipped off? Jake bent over, looking beneath him in every direction. How could she have simply disappeared?

Before the carousel came to a complete stop, he slid from his steed, stood at the edge of the ride, still searching for Katlyn.

"Where is she?" he yelled to the attendant. "My friend, did you see where she went?" Jake jumped off the platform and approached the man. "You had to have seen her get off the carousel."

"I'm sorry sir." The gatekeeper looked at him with consternation. "I saw no woman. Perhaps the spinning confused you."

"Are you crazy?" Jake scowled at the man. "You spoke to her. Katlyn rode right beside me. I held her hand through the whole ride, but . . ." He scanned the area, scratching his head. "It's like she vanished."

The man shut down the motor, turned off the flashing lights. "Perhaps your friend needed to leave." He stepped back onto the ride and began to wipe down the horses, then looked over his shoulder at Jake. "You could always check with the security guards in the cabin near the entrance." With an enigmatic smile, he turned back to his task.

"Right." Jake scanned the area, rubbing the stubbles on his chin. Get a grip, Jake. There had to be a logical explanation and panicking wouldn't help him find her. He pulled out his cell phone. "Call Katlyn Harris," he spoke into the microphone as he walked toward the midway. Her number rang repeatedly, but she didn't pick up. Remembering the picture he'd taken earlier, he scrolled to his photos and wandered toward the security hut.

"If she was a young-in, it'd be different. She probably just took off to soothe her ruffled feathers."

"For the last time, we weren't fighting." Jake's tone was laced with annoyance. "Can I at least get someone to help me look for her? She has to be here somewhere."

"Women. Ya never know what they're thinkin'. You probably said something innocent that set her off."

"No. We were riding the carousel and...oh never mind. I'll find her myself." Jake stormed out of the cabin. "Rent-a-cops," he grumbled, shaking his head.

He searched the entire park, showing Katlyn's picture to employees and random patrons alike, asking if anyone had seen his friend. After covering every square inch of the carnival, he reluctantly returned to the Miata. Glancing down at his watch, he wondered if he should call the police, or would they think him mad to report a disappearance less than an hour old? They would surely tell him to wait at least twenty-four.

His mind reeling, Jake drove back to her house, thinking about Kat, the first time he'd met her and how oddly incredible their relationship had been. Perhaps she would be there when he arrived. She simply couldn't have vanished without a trace. He'd been right next to her and he knew in his gut she would never just leave. Something happened, but what?

When he pulled into the driveway, he glanced at the empty boxes neatly stacked against the curb. He hadn't imagined the day he'd spent with her. He'd helped Kat unpack her things, set up her bed, and put her kitchen table together. Riddled with angst, he parked, leapt up the porch steps, then unlocked the door and called out to her.

"Katlyn, are you here?" His voice echoed through the emptiness. He ran room-to-room, calling her, searching the house first, then the grounds. Baffled, Jake wandered into the kitchen, opened the fridge and stared blankly at its contents. He wasn't hungry. But he could use a stiff drink. He strolled into the parlor, hoping to find some triple malt whisky or the makings for a dry martini, but Katlyn didn't indulge in spirits often. A glass of fine wine was more her style. He walked behind the wet bar, then smiled. Brandy, Cognac, to be specific. That would do.

He reached for a snifter next to the wine glasses that hung from a rack on the back wall, poured a shot of brandy then swirled it around before sipping. The smooth liquid burned as it flowed down his throat and he immediately felt the warmth in his stomach. Grabbing the snifter in one hand, the bottle in the other, he ambled across the room, collapsed onto the sofa, his mind still focused on Kat. How could he find out what had happened to her? He was a smart man, resourceful. There had to be a way. Contemplating his cognac, he sipped while wracking his brain.

Now, somewhat inebriated, Jake's mind drifted back to his youth. Unlike Katlyn, he'd had a wonderful childhood, a close-knit family surrounded by love. Of course they had their share of sibling rivalry, but his brother Brian was his best friend and they both adored and protected Alyssa, their baby sister. Katlyn had grown up alone, shuffled between foster homes, while Jake's life had flourished.

His parents had been terrific role models, more in love now than the day they married. But the core of the family was his grandparents. They had a love for the ages. He'd heard their story over-and-over as a child and never tired of it, a magical tale of chivalry, perseverance, and unbridled love that beat every movie he'd seen or book he'd read.

His gran's stories captivated all who heard them. Whether of castles and kings or vampire tales, her writing enticed every reader's mind or listening ears. But Gran had held sacred the unpublished tales of family lore, volumes of remarkable stories that kept her grandchildren completely enthralled.

Though it had been months since Papa and Gran had passed away, Jake still felt their presence, especially Gran's. But he knew they'd had a wonderful life together and had died peacefully within days of each other.

Jake set the snifter down on the coffee table, walked out to his truck. Reaching behind the back seat, he pulled out an old family album he'd brought to show Kat, to share his family with her. Picking up the worn scrapbook, he held it close to his chest and returned to his bottle of brandy.

He ran his hand over the book, opened it to the first page, a faded snapshot of Papa and Gran on their wedding day. Page-by-page, Jake examined the photos, remembering tales he'd heard as a boy and treasured memories of his own childhood. The old black and white pictures of Papa and Gran told a story of a passionate love affair and the family that had blossomed from it. Jake hoped to find his soul mate one day and build a story of his own, but for the past year, Kat's happiness had come first.

"Kat..." His voice came out in a whisper. "Where are you?"

He closed the scrapbook, placed it on the coffee table in front of him. There had to be something he could do. A rush of anxiety surged down his spine and, running his fingers through his hair, he stood, grabbed his drink, then strolled toward the hearth.

The painting, a simple landscape of the back yard, had enchanted Kat. He took a swig of brandy, then moved in closer to study the canvas ...the snifter dropped from his hand, crashed to the floor. Jake didn't flinch. Instead, he stared in disbelief.

She had spoken to him across time through the brush strokes of an artist's hand. She hadn't been there before when Kat first showed him the landscape. He'd seen the lake, the stone bench, and the lonely young man. But now the picture had changed. The portrait of a solitary man sitting on the bench in the foreground of the lake setting had transformed into one of a man and woman on their wedding day, their hands and hearts clearly entwined. Jake moved in closer, inspected the couple.

"Kat," he whispered again.

A year before they died, Gran and Papa had called Jake to their side and told him a remarkable story. Since then, Gran had recounted it frequently, explaining every detail save one. Their story sounded bizarre, impossible. And the things the two of them had asked him to do were eccentric at best, teetering on the verge of senility. At first Jake had shrugged them off, but Gran had been so insistent.

They knew their health was failing. Perhaps their minds were waning, too. One would expect that of ninety-year-olds. It didn't matter though. Jake knew they truly believed every word they'd told him, and he owed them so much. As unusual as their requests seemed, the proposals weren't dangerous. What harm would it do to humor his beloved, ailing grandparents?

Gran said that Katlyn was a distant relative, told him where to find her, how to meet and befriend her, insisting that Kat must find happiness before Jake could find his own. Until the day she died, Gran had begged her grandchild to tell her everything about the woman and wanted constant updates.

"Promise me this one thing," Gran had said. "And tell no one, not even Katlyn."

Jake promised.

With stage-four lung cancer, Papa had transferred everything into Gran's name, expecting she would outlive him. And she did, but once Papa passed, she lost the sparkle that Papa had placed in her eyes.

Her frail body gave up and within a week, she had slipped away too. For a whole year prior to their passing, Jake had known that Katlyn Harris would inherit their home with everything in it upon Gran's death. He would deliver the will, telling Kat nothing about Kathrin, especially the fact that he was her grandson.

Now Jake finally understood why. As bizarre as their story had been, Gran and Papa had told him the truth. Now Jake could let go. Touching the canvas, he ran his fingers over the woman in the painting—over the portrait of Kat. Somehow her white winged-horse had taken her back in time to find Collin Morgan, the love of her life.

After cleaning up the broken glass, Jake grabbed another snifter and poured some more brandy. Sitting back down on the sofa, he pulled a manila folder from the back of his scrapbook. It was finally time to open Gran's envelope. He slid his fingers inside the flap breaking the seal, took out a single sheet of paper, then read his grandmother's final request:

Codicil to the Last Will and Testament
Kathrin Elizabeth Morgan

In the event that Katlyn E. Harris for any reason cannot be present for the second reading of my will to be held in my home on 14 February, 2013, I hereby bequeath my property, house, and the contents left therein to my grandson, Jacob Daniel Morgan, for services he provided me beyond the realm of anything one could imagine. Thank you my dear Jake for fulfilling our destiny.

Love forever, Gran.

Jake folded the letter and placed it on the table, picked up his cognac, then walked back to the hearth and Kat's painting. He finally had the ending to Gran's remarkable story, or more accurately, the beginning. Smiling, he pulled out his cell phone and scrolled to the picture he'd taken of Kat earlier that morning and noticed he'd caught her painting as well. Enlarging the photo, he smiled, gaping at the solitary man sitting alone on the stone bench. It was you all the time, Papa.

He looked up at Kat's portrait. Raising his glass, he shook his head in wonderment. "To you, Gran," he whispered. "I promised you this morning that I'd stay with you until I knew you were happy. And now I know. You had a wonderful life, Kat." Jake smiled. "I'm honored that you trusted me enough to help you go back in time to find your true love.

Kathrin Elizabeth Harris Morgan had finally returned to the arms of her soul mate, Collin. Destiny had been set straight in the circle of life. And the mysterious hidden painting had been Gran's message in a bottle of sorts, not to Katlyn, but rather to tell her beloved grandson, Jake, that she'd finally found happiness.

Casi McLean

Books

Casi McLean

A Note From Casi

I hope you enjoyed my series and if you did, please leave an Amazon review. They help authors more than you could imagine.

Look for my novels. My newest series, Lake Lanier Mysteries, is a three-book time-slip romantic suspense inspired by creepy lore and supernatural legends attached to Atlanta's famous man-made Lake Lanier.

Each novel is stand-alone, but some characters carry into subsequent stories. Beneath The Lake, book one, Beyond The Mist, book two, and Between The Shadows, book three, bond together in a cyclone of mystery haunting Lake Lanier, while thrusting characters through the fabric of time.

The next few pages reveal a sneak peek of Lake Lanier Mysteries and more of my books:

Beneath The Lake

After discovering her boyfriend's affair, Lacey Montgomery peels away into the throes of a torrential storm, spins out of control and hurls into the depths of an icy, black, lake. She awakens in the arms of a handsome stranger, in a place she's never heard of, thirty-four years before she was born.

When the 2012 lawyer meets the 1949 hunk, fire and ice swirl into a stream of sweltering desire. Bobby is captivated the moment the storm-ravaged woman opened her eyes. Trapped in a web of betrayal set in motion by her father's rejection, Lacey swears off men, but the charming Bobby Reynolds stirs her passion.

The desperation to find her way home dissolves as Lacey falls in love with a town destined to be erased from the face of the Earth, and the man who vows to protect his heritage. Will they discover the cryptic key to a mysterious portal before time rips them apart? Or will their sprits wander forever through a ghost town buried beneath the lake?

Find Beneath The Lake on Amazon

http://amzn.to/2tadLyz

Watch The Trailer:

https://www.youtube.com/watch?v=TwOqm8DUUfA

Beneath The Lake

Chapter One
Lake Lanier, GA ~ June 2011

A final thud hurled him backwards, flailing through brush and thickets like a rag doll. Grasping at anything to break momentum, Rob's hand clung to a branch wedged into the face of the precipice. Spiny splinters sliced his skin. Oozing blood trickled into his palms and, one by one, his fingers slowly slipped.

A sharp crack echoed through the silence of the ravine as the bough succumbed to his weight. He plummeted into free-fall. Clenching his eyes, he drew in a deep breath, terrified of the pain, the mauling that waited on the jagged rocks below.

When icy water broke his fall, the chill kept him from losing consciousness. He swirled, straining to see, but darkness enveloped him. Soggy clothing pulled him deeper-- deeper into the murky, fathomless depths. He wrestled to squirm free from the waterlogged jacket dragging him down to a watery grave, watched the coat disappear into black obscurity.

Panic clenched his stomach, or was it death that snaked around his chest, squeezing, squeezing, squeezing the air, the life from his body? Lack of oxygen burned his lungs, beckoning surrender and a chard of rage pierced his gut as reality set in. He lunged upward with one last thrust and burst from the water's deadly grip, gasping for air. A gurgling howl spewed from depths of his soul and echoed into silence.

Sunlight shimmered across a smooth, indigo lake, but aside from the slight ripples of his own paddling, nothing but stillness surrounded him. He floated toward the shore, sucking deep breaths into his lungs until the pummeling in his chest subsided. When he reached the water's edge, he hoisted his body onto the soft red clay and collapsed while the sun's warmth drained the tension from his body.

No one knew he had survived. The rules had shifted--he mused--now he could reinvent himself, become a stealth predator. His target: Lacey Madison Montgomery.

Beyond The Mist

When a treacherous storm spirals Piper Taylor into the arms of Nick Cramer, an intriguing lawyer, she never expects to fall in love. But when he disappears, she risks her life to find him, unaware the search will thrust her into international espionage, terrorism, and the space-time continuum.

Nick leads a charmed life except when it comes to his heart. Haunted by a past relationship, he can't move forward with Piper despite the feelings she evokes. When he stumbles upon a secret portal hidden beneath Atlanta's Lake Lanier, he seizes the chance to correct his mistakes.

A slip through time has consequences beyond their wildest dreams. Can Piper find Nick and bring him home before he alters the fabric of time, or will the lovers drift forever Beyond The Mist?

Beyond The Mist

Chapter One
Lake Lanier, GA June 2012

A soft mist hovered over the moonlit lake, beckoning, luring him forward with the seductive enticement of a mermaid's song. Rhythmic clatter of a distant train moaned in harmony with a symphony of cricket chirps and croaking frogs. Spellbound, Nick Cramer took a long breath and waded deeper into the murky cove.

Dank air, laden with a scent of soggy earth and pine, crawled across his bare arms. The hairs on the back of his neck bristled, shooting a prickle down his spine that slithered into an icy pool coiled in the pit of his stomach. He clenched his fingers into a tight fist, determined to fight through the emotion consuming him. Fear sliced through his belly like icy shards until he finally heaved, forcing rancid bile to choke into his throat.

I have to do this--he inched forward--*only a few more steps and*--a sudden surge swirled around him, yanking him into a whirling vortex, where a violent blue streak dragged him deeper, deeper beneath the lake into shadowy depths. Heart pounding, he battled against the force, twisting, pulling toward the surface with all of his strength but, despite his muscular build, he spun like a feather in wind into oblivion. When the mist dissolved, Nick Cramer had vanished...

Between The Shadows

Chapter One
At the base of the Chestatee River, North Georgia, May 24, 1865

Bella wiggled her toes in the squishy mud. A cool trickle seeped through, soothing her swollen feet. She loved sitting by the water's edge, watching the ebb and flow sparkle reflected sunbeams across the river. But today necessity took precedence over pleasure. Her very life held in the balance. She squeezed her eyes, drawing in a deep breath filled with the scent of spring flowers drifting on the breeze. Holding the air a moment before slowly releasing, she centered her thoughts.

In the distance, pounding hooves tromped across firm Georgia clay, breaking through the mid-morning silence. Stiffening at the approaching danger, she pressed splayed fingers against the ground to gage the threat. She listened, attentive to their pace and direction. The hoof beats were closing in despite her evasive tactics. Shadowing the creek to confuse her pursuers averted capture, but only briefly. She had little time for pampering wounds or resting tired legs. She must forge ahead with haste.

Scooping cool water over her feet, Bella rinsed away soft sludge comforting the blisters that burned and bit at her toes. She blotted the dampness then winced in pain. Thankful she *borrowed* more suitable apparel from a random clothesline and abandoned her crinolines when she took to the road, she hastily ripped her undergarment into strips and wrapped the tender injuries. Then, wasting no time, she snatched the clothes from the bushes where she'd spread them to dry, pulled a linen shirt over her head, and tucked the long hem into heavy denim trousers before slipping into her tattered, brown leather shoes.

The sentinels following her would have no pity on a spy despite the wiles of feminine charm she could conjure when necessary. A chill quivered down her arms at a fleeting vision of her lifeless body, dangling from a noose, the rope stretched over a branch of an old oak tree. Whether she intended to be a spy or not proved irrelevant. Her blood streamed with inherent curiosity and passion, sealing her fate.

Bending to one knee, Bella quickly splashed water on her face then wiped her sleeve across her cheeks. She ran her damp fingers through her hair and, threading her locks into a fat braid, she tucked and pulled until the mound sat snuggly under her gray cap. Instinctively cinching her trouser tie, she paused then let the waistband slack again. If captured, she didn't want her small waist to reveal her gender. Worse fates existed than dangling from the end of a rope.

She listened again before darting through the forest in the opposite direction from the men trailing her. Farther, farther until her chest hurt and she could run no more. Slowing her stride to catch her breath, she pushed ahead as far as she could bear. Her feet burned with pain, compelling her to halt, if only for a moment. She leaned against a willow tree and drew in several long, silent breaths.

A crack in the brushwood gave warning. Bella snapped around. Sunlight pierced through branches above, catching a glint of silver-white. A sparkle reflected off a bayonet as the weapon's owner squinted, his gaze cast upward. She edged behind a bush and crouched, her heart thumping wildly, her breath trapped within the knot in her throat.

A soft crunch rustled behind her, and a hand slid over her mouth and nose. Bella had no time to counter. She screamed--but no sound escaped the suffocating grip. No plea for help. No air. Squirming and yanking, she struggled, desperate to free herself, but to no avail. Trapped body to body, she fought for air, unable to see her assailant. The odor of sweat laced with tobacco and spirits heaved her stomach, causing the whirling in her head to spin faster and deeper, until the sunlight narrowed into tiny stars against a midnight sky--then faded into darkness...

Wingless Butterfly
Healing The Broken Child Within

"You don't want to know him. He's the kind of man who pulls wings off of butterflies."

Her mother's warning haunted her through a childhood steeped in mystery, and sparked a domino effect reflecting what she perceived was true. Until she uncovered secrets and lies in her past that changed everything.

A TRANSFORMATIONAL SELF-HELP MEMOIR

Wingless Butterfly shares a lifetime of secrets like whispers from a best friend and unveils the metamorphosis of a broken child, her struggle to escape a silken chrysalis cocooning her heart, and her desperation to find love, validation, and self-worth. When the mist of a new dawn settled, the fragmented little girl emerged confident and secure with wings to fly in a whole new world--that child was me.

Intimate stories linger within each of us; a unique saga that is ours alone with twists, turns, hopes, and dreams. Some people thrive on messages perceived through childhood; others splinter. But as different as each individual may seem, we all love, hurt, and bleed the same. The distinctiveness of our past develops who we become.

So can we change and, if so, is it possible to erase a lifetime of beliefs? Perspective is reality. When I shattered the broken reflection in the mirror of my past, I finally healed and followed my dreams.

This is my story.
Find Wingless Butterfly on Amazon:
http://amzn.to/2u4bJow

About Casi McLean

Award winning author, Casi McLean, pens novels to stir the soul with romance, suspense, and a sprinkle of magic. Her writing crosses genres from ethereal, captivating shorts with eerie twist endings to believable time slips, mystical plots, and sensual romantic suspense, like Beneath The Lake, WINNER: 2016 Gayle Wilson Award of Excellence for BEST Romantic Suspense.

Casi's powerful memoir, Wingless Butterfly: Healing The Broken Child Within, shares an inspirational message of courage, tenacity, and hope, and displays her unique ability to excel in nonfiction and self-help as well as fiction. Known for enchanting stories with magical description, McLean entices readers in nonfiction as well with fascinating hooks to hold them captive in storylines they can't put down.

Her romance entwines strong, believable heroines with delicious hot heroes to tempt the deepest desires then fans the flames, sweeping readers into their innermost romantic fantasies.

Ms. McLean weaves exceptional romantic mystery with suspenseful settings and lovable characters you'll devour. You'll see, hear, and feel the magical eeriness of one fateful night. You'll swear her time travel could happen, be mystified by her other worldly images, and feel heat of romantic suspense, but most of all you'll want more.

Find all her books on her Amazon Page:

http://amzn.to/2ueP8G0

www.ingramcontent.com/pod-product-compliance
Lightning Source LLC
Chambersburg PA
CBHW020914180626
46816CB00007BA/2391